Her Fate

....

Chloe Pinsel

Contents

D rapetomania (n.)- The overwhelming urge to run away

Aurelia Moreno

A voice said, "Good morning, Aurelia. It's time for you to get up."

As I turned away from the person, I mumbled, "Five minutes more."

"Since it is already morning, you must get up. Your parents are already waiting for you downstairs "With a chuckle, the voice added.I'm surprised. When I look around, I notice a maid smiling at me.

"Come on, they've been waiting for a long time. You don't want them to be kept waiting, do you?" She remarked, pointing to the clock on my room's wall. What do these people expect from me so early in the morning? It's fucking eight o'clock in the morning.

"Can I have 5 more minutes to wake up?" I inquire, pulling my blanket over my head to shield my face from the brightness of the light streaming into my bedroom.

"OK," she says as she moves towards the door, "but please be downstairs in no more than twenty minutes." She added while taking the doorhandle and stepping out into the hallway.But, before shutting the door, she smiled and said, "Your parents are waiting." She then exited my room, closing the door.

I grumble as I stand up and enter my bathroom. I quickly get ready and then choose and put on my clothing. I emerged from my room and proceeded down the stairs to the kitchen, where I observed the cook preparing a wonderful breakfast.

"Morning, can you please prepare me some maple syrup pancakes and a fruit dish this morning?" I inquired, and he nodded. I was ready to leave when it dawned to me, "Oh, and don't forget the extra tiny pancakes." I grinned and exited the kitchen, entering the dining room.

"Good morning, Aurelia," my father says, his smile covered behind his hand as he swallows some pastry.

"Morning," I murmur grumpily as I settle into my chair and gaze out the window, at New York's beautiful scenery. I could see the sun beaming and hear the bustling streets. We resided in the heart of Manhattan, with a stunning view of some of the city's highlights. Though it was much busier here than in Queens or Brooklyn.

"Aurelia," my father sternly said. "huh?" I inquired, my gaze fixed on him. He indicated to a maid standing next to me, holding my breakfast. "Thank you," I said as I smiled at her and took it from her. She lowered her head and smiled before heading to the kitchen.

"You need to be more aware of your surroundings. What if there's a prospective assailant nearby who wants to stab you? However, you are more concerned with the weather than with your surroundings." my father stated.

"She has only recently awoken, Leo. Before you criticize her, give her a chance to wake up." Looking at my father, my mother remarked. In every crisis, my mother has always been there for me.She was a typical girl living in a little apartment with her lovely family in France before she got into the mafia business, because of my father. To be honest, her family was wealthy, but it didn't appear to bother her.

I've met a lot of rich girls my age, but they're mostly boring. Except for one girl, whose name I can't recall; I had a crush on her, but her family moved away from America to another nation whose name I can't quite remember. She was absolutely adorable and we used to have a lot of fun when we were children; now she must be somewhere around 18 years old, the same age as me, and most likely has a boyfriend.Yes, I knew she didn't like girls from the beginning.

Dad hurriedly slammed his lips shut. In silence, we finish the last bites of breakfast. I got up and went to the gym once I finished. I needed to work out a little more. I haven't done much in the last several months, so my body is weaker, and we have a mission coming up in a few days, most likely tomorrow, so I need to catch up if I want to participate.

☐

When my Mother entered the gym, I had already been working out for almost an hour. She gave me a friendly smile and motioned for me to continue. I came to a halt and removed my headphones.

"Mom?" I questioned as I wiped the sweat from my forehead with a towel.

She chuckled and said, "I just wanted to see you." Something had to have happened.

"Well, either way, I was done." I remarked it as I approached her and sat down. "What are your true desires, Mom?" I let out a sigh.

"Nothing but watching my own child do what she enjoys. Isn't it possible for a mother to do just that?" She gave me a kind smile. Working out isn't my favorite activity, but it kept me engaged, which was beneficial.

"All right, I'm going to take a shower and then we'll chat, okay?" She nodded as I sighed. I hurriedly showered in the ensuite bathroom. Then I changed into something more comfortable and returned to the gym, only to find my mother sitting on one of the couches.

"So, what do you want to talk about?" I ask as I take a seat next to her.

She shrugged and said, "Nothing, just wanted to see you."

I deadpanned and turned to face her, saying, "Mom, I know you." She appeared to be an exact replica of me, or rather, I appeared to be an exact replica of her. When I was a baby, I looked more like my father, but as I grew older, I began to resemble my mother.

Her dark brown hair was laying across her shoulders, and her chocolate brown eyes were watching me intently. Mom had a fantastic sense of style and preferred to dress in more modern attire with a hint of glamour. "Anyway, I've got to get going." As she stood up and walked upstairs, she smiled at me. As she does so, I give her a pleasant smile.

"Aurelia, we have to discuss about the mission," my father says as he walks in. Standing up, I ask, "Yes, Dad?"

"Come along with me. Do we would really want to talk here?" He motions for me to take the stairwell towards his office. I followed him, and we arrived shortly after.

As other men entered the room, I sat down next to him in the chair.

02

N epenthe (n: Nuh-Pen-Thee) - Something that can make you forget grief or suffering

Aurelia Moreno

As other men entered the room, I walked into the office and sat down next to my father.

My father spoke up as everyone was inside and the door was finally closed "As you are all aware, tomorrow will be one of our most important missions. We'll attempt to eliminate Ivanov, also known as Nikolai. As you are all knowing, he is the cousin of the Russian mafia boss." "Dad," he continued "However, we require assistance. So I requested the Italians, who will be present tomorrow."

Not the Italians. I groaned quietly to myself. They annoy me. Luciano was a real jerk the first time I met him.

Throwback

"Leonardo" Lorenzo, the Italian Mafia Leader nodded.

Dad returned the nod and said, "Lorenzo."

Then we all sat down and started talking about business. I found this part of the mafia business to really be tiresome, so I tried to pass the time by looking around the room until I was interrupted by a boy who stood in my way.

"Can you tell me what you're looking at?" "You have nothing to look at around here," he said rudely. He made sure that I was just focused on the meeting for the rest of the meeting.

Dad and his father said their goodbyes to us later that day, when we were finished. "Goodbye, and I hope you don't look around so rudely in other private areas in the future," he replies angrily.

"Why do you even care in the slightest?" I respond with a sassy question.

"Why wouldn't I, it was my home you looked around in," he shrugged.

We argued for a while longer until we were interrupted by our Dads. "Aurelia say bye to Lorenzo" Dad said sharply. "Goodbye," I said with a smile.

He grinned back and said, "Bye, have a wonderful evening Aurelia."

Then we drove back to our house.

Throwback's end

I really hate him.

Though Sofia, Lorenzo's only daughter and his second child, was someone I liked. When we were kids, we even became really good friends and played a lot together. But Luciano is someone I've never really met before. I only saw him this one time. He was apparently enrolled in some sort of private school or whatever. After that incident, I continued to meet up with Sofia.

Victoria, his mother, was also a sweetheart. When I came over, she would always bake us cookies and let us watch as many movies as we wanted as long as it wasn't past bedtime. Victoria would also let us go to the beach, which was only a few minutes away from their home. I adored their home; it reminded me of my childhood, as Mom and Victoria were great friends, therefore we spent most summers there.

"So, guys, I'd like to meet up with you at 6 a.m. tomorrow. Here. Then we'll go into the details." The gathering was called to an end by Dad. All of the men left the office and went somewhere else. I stayed behind since I knew my father wanted to speak with me in private.

"I want you to be on your best behavior tomorrow, Aurelia," Dad said.

"But-" I tried to interject.

"No, no, no. This is a business related mission. With the Italians, we can't make a mistake. They've become far more powerful than you understand." He put an end to the conversation. Dad stood up and headed to the door, picking up some of the folders, lying on his desk. He fixed his gaze on me as I sat motionless on my chair. He motioned to the door and said, "You can go now, Aurelia."

I stood up and went to my room. I swear to God, if Luciano can't maintain a pleasant behavoir, neither can I.

It's as simple as that.

I enter my room, which is ideally suited to my needs. I have a sofa next to my bookcases, which include some of my favorite books. Then there's my bed, as well as my vanity and mirror. I also have a walk-in closet and an ensuite bathroom, which I appreciate because I have so many clothing.

I went into my closet and first chose a good clothing for tomorrow, or rather, several good outfits. We have an all black, with black dressing pants, a black sexy top and black high heels. A dark red velvet dress with one slit to show off my calf and a v-neck, along with dark green high heels.A mini black dress with black high heels and a black shoulder bag. Or black mom jeans, a black tight fitting shirt and some black boots.

"Hey, Mom, do you need any assistance?" I inquire, smiling at her.

"Thank you, honey," I say. "Could you please bring the plates and dial your Dad's number?" she asked.

"Of course," I say and I smiled as I walked to my father's office, only to come to a halt at the door "Oh, and one more thing before I forget. What's for dinner tonight?" I wonder.

"Well, you'll find out soon enough. Don't you agree?" She laughed and motioned for me to fetch my father down so that we could finally eat.

I dash up the stairs and hear him on the phone with someone. Normally, I would never do something like that, but who hasn't secretly listened in on their parents' phone calls as a child? I pressed my ear on the door to hear what they were saying. I couldn't understand anything at first, but then I realized my Father was talking to someone I didn't quiet know.

"Yea, okay, we can do that," my Father said, then paused for a moment before continuing, "Yea, our businesses will merge."

Well, I don't think I was expected to hear that. He would never ever merge his business with someone, it's to important to him. "Dad Dinner is ready," I said as I knocked on the door. I thought I overheard him say something.

He answered, "Yes Aurelia, I'll be down in a few minutes," and I nodded and walked downstairs.What was he referring to?

This chapter is edited

03

E ramnesia (n: Eee-Rom-Nee-Sha) - The realization of being born in the wrong time period and wishing to live another.

Aurelia Moreno

It was the next day, exactly 10am. We've just had the morning meeting to discuss the details. And of course the De Lucas, the Italian Mafia, was there too. Sadly only Lorenzo and Luciano and some of their men.

Dad told us all what his plan is. Basically I should attract Nikolai so he would follow me to some private room or the best situation outside. Some Men will be with me inside who will watch that I'm good and not going to be hurt. After he has come with me, we will kill him or take him with us, depends on what the best thing to do is in the situation we are in.

Just to clarify, I'll not kill him. I'm a Mafia kid but I'm not doing such thing till I have to. And that's clearly not the case.

My Dad also told us where we are going, apparently my Father had opened a new club in the city, where Nikolai goes very often to, he's one of the Regular customers there which comes by daily. So we just hope that he will be there today too.

I'm currently sitting in my room, thinking what outfit would be the best and I decide to take the mini black dress with black high heels with the black shoulder bag. I put everything on and locked at myself in the mirror. Apart from my hair and makeup, I looked sexy. I would definitely get some mens attentions.

I smiled at myself and went to my dressing table and did my makeup. I did some natural basic makeup, so I looked a bit younger. I had to, apparently he likes younger girls more and between both of our ages is only one year. So that not pretty much enough. With my makeup on I looked basically two years younger than I am.

Which is 16. Now that's not so legal but who cares, you do much illegal things when you're in the mafia.

After finishing my makeup I try to do something with my hair. I fixed it a bit firstly and then curled it a bit so it looked okay.

I looked stunning, if I could say so. My hair was looking good, my makeup wasn't as smeared as the last days and the outfit I wore was fitting well with my body. After some looking into the mirror and fixing my hair a bit I went downstairs, to meet my fathers and somebody else's eyes staring at me.

Firstly I didn't know who they were but after looking at them a little closer I could see Lorenzo and Luciano watching me walking down these stairs. I saw Lucianos eyes roaming my body like he owns it, which made me a bit uncomfortable.

As I got down the stairs the eyes never left my body, I had to cough a little to get the attention from my body to my face, which was way more pleasant.

"So, I'm ready." I state, turning to my Dad, who hums in agreement. He looks at Lorenzo and Luciano and both of them nod and turn around to walk to the car.

Two cars stood outside. Luciano got into the first one and Lorenzo in the second. I was just about to ask which one I should take when my Dad cut me off.

"You will drive with Luciano. Lorenzo and I will be directly at the back entrance with the car, just if there is any emergency. If it's all going as planned then you won't even need us. Do you understand?" He explains to me, I just nod. He can't leave me alone with this fucking bastard.

My Dad took me to the car and opened the door for me. He helped me inside as he hold one of my hands. "Have a nice ride" He smiles at me and Luciano.

"Thanks Dad" I forced a smile at him. I thought he would close the door, but before he did so he pointed at me and Luciano just blankly nodded his head. What do they know that I don't?

We drove off to the club ,as I looked out the window to look at the beautiful star sky. Today was a beautiful night, not rainy nor cloudy and the beautiful looking stars were shining as bright as they could. You could also get a clear look at the moon, it was a full moon. Guess who is not going to get an eye closed tonight!

The car took a hold and I looked out of the window. We were already there, I didn't thought that we would be that fast. Luciano opened his door and got out first. Just as I wanted to open mine, someone came me before and opened it. I couldn't see them because of a streetlight blinding me. The not known person gave me their hand for me to get out of the car. I gladly took it and stepped out.

And there I saw him, it was Luciano who was such a gentleman. I murmured a quick , "Thank you" and forced me out of his stare, which was lingering on me. I didn't know this club, as it was new, but Dad has talked to me about it a while ago while they planned building it. And to be honest it looked even more stunning then on all the pre-models which he showed me. I walked towards the entrance and could still feel his eyes on my back, watching every step I did.

I got to the Bouncer at the door and showed him my ID. I smile at him brightly, no-one of the employees know me personally and have never seen me. They all just know that their boss has one daughter and that's it. I understand that he did it for my own safety but it still feels like he is a little ashamed of me.

He probably wanted a son first, so he could take the business over. But that never happened, and it won't ever. My Mother had many miscarriages after my birth, she clearly suffered which you could still see today. But she was also happy, about me that I was born. My Dad is a Dad you could say, he was protective over me since the day I was born and when he was told that Mom couldn't have any children anymore he was way more protective.

Everything I did outside ,out of his eyes, had to be reported to him. He started an early training with me, so that I could defend myself and had only the best assigns assist me, well it didn't really help. When I was five and was attending a ball with my Mother and Father, one of my fathers Mafia enemy kidnapped me and kept me for three days. These were the worst three days of my life, even though they didn't do anything to me.

The Bouncer looked me up and down and then wished me a great stay and let me in. Oh I will have it.

04

Monophobia (n: Mon-Oh-Phobia) - The fear of being alone or being left alone

Aurelia Moreno

The Bouncer looked me up and down and then wished me a great stay and let me in. Oh I will have it.

I get inside and firstly looked for my target. And there he was sitting on one of the many bar stools drinking what looked like some type of beer, clearly drunk already. Why the fuck would he be drunk already, I bet that he only had beer since he showed up here? He was enjoying himself, laughing about something one of his men said. A woman walked towards him and directly sat down on his lap. She didn't look somewhat like his wife, which I've seen many times at events of the mafia.

The woman grinned her ass down on his lap and moved her hips in circles, clearly getting his dick hard. I disgust at the fact that I'm about to sit there, the same place this woman sits right now and do the same thing or something directly the same. I saw how he whispered something in her ear and she abruptly stood up. They walked towards what I think is the private area ,my Dad showed me this morning.

After some deadly bored minutes, of just standing there and looking around. I ordered myself some Gin and headed over to the bar he was currently sitting at. I could smell the sweat from afar, disgusting. I pushed the thoughts and smell to the side and walked straight towards him. I swayed my hips seductively, he smiled as soon as he caught the site of me. I smile back and sit down on his lap, and grinned my ass on his bulge. He puts his arms around me and whispered something in Russian, which I didn't understand.

"Давай повеселимся, тебе не кажется, дорогая? - Let's have some fun, don't you think Sweetheart?" He said his voice only hearable for me. Nikolai bit my earlobe and I packed a moan. He picked me up and walked towards the private area, bingo that's right where I wanted him to be. "Одна комната, и поторопитесь, мы не хотим, чтобы женщина ждала! - One room, and hurry up we don't want to let the woman wait!" his voice increased a bit at the employee who looked scared at him. He rummaged through a box and handed Ivanov some keys.

"Let's go котенок, давай повеселимся - kitten, let's have some fun." He took me to the last room of the hallway and opened the door, and closed it after us. He firstly looked at me seductively and the began with pushing the sleeves of my dress off so that my bra could be seen, he drooled at the sight of it. Please Dad hurry up.

I tried to push him off, but no success. Ivanov pushed me onto the bed and took my hands above my head.

Nikolai continued by taking my bra off. "Please stop" I whimper, but he didn't stop. Soon my breast were on display and he didn't take a second and took them in his mouth. "Stop it" I cry out and exactly this moment the door was thrown to the ground and Dad, Lorenzo and Luciano stood there with many De Luca Men.

"Let her go" Dad roared and send some men to cover the room. Ivanov quickly stood back and looked at my father who was red with anger. I tried cover up as quick as I could, so that I wouldn't be half naked in front of them. Lorenzo and Luciano didn't halt a second and put him on the ground beating his face, as my father comes running for me. "Are you ok darling?" He asked helping me up.

I tried to stand but my legs had other ideas and buckled as soon as they hit the ground. Dad helped me standing and placed me onto the bed. He let me sit there and watch how they brutally beat the shit out of Nikolai, who just lays on the ground groaning. "You'll never ever touch my daughter again!" My Dad roared at the same time beating Ivanov up. He soon was in and out of fainting and some De Luca Men took him with them, where ever they are going.

"Luciano take her with you and bring her back home. She needs time." Dad said still red with anger, trying to control his rage. Luciano didn't say a word and came towards me, while Dad and Lorenzo left the room. He picked me up bridal style and brought me out of the room into the hallway where more Men were waiting for us, which I could just make up because of my blurry vision. Luciano walked in the front and some men were following us.

"Clean this mess up in there. We don't want anyone to see this!" He said to one of his men, who quickly took out his phone and dialed a number. He talked while walking next to us, there was silent nobody said anything only hearable were their steps.

"They will be here in five minutes Luciano" The Man said to Luciano, who just nodded his head. He walked towards a car and opened the passenger door, put me inside and went towards the drivers door. Tears were still escaping my eyes, I was exhausted and couldn't even keep my eyes open. I heard how the door was opened and the engine was brought to live. And then the darkness took over.

Luciano

Her Father ordered me to take her home, which I did. I was still in daze, picked her up bridal style and went outside were more of my Men stood, guarding the hallway. I could still hear her whimpers as she played exhausted in my arms. Even though I hate her it made my heart break.

"Clean this mess up in there. We don't want anyone to see this!" I said to Marco, who is one of my sotto-capos. He quickly took out his phone and dialed a number. He talked while walking next to us, there was silent nobody said anything only hearable were our steps and her soft whimpers.

"They will be here in five minutes Luciano" Marco, I just nodded and walked with Aurelia towards a car. I opened the passenger door and put her inside. I went towards the drivers seat and started the engine, after making sure that she had her seatbelt on. I saw how she fell asleep within seconds and drove fast towards their apartment which was in middle of Manhattan. The streets were busy ,at this time of the day many people want to go home from parties or work.

I drive into the underground garage of the building and parked in one of the free parking spots. I got out and picked her up. A car stopped next to me, three guards came out of it and accompanied me brining her to her apartment. I went into the elevator and as soon as we arrive at their penthouse her mother came running towards us. She had tears in her eyes and was crying hysterically.

"AURELIA" she cried as she saw her daughter in my arms sleeping with dry tears covering her cheeks. "No no no no no" she cried.

"I will bring her to her room if you don't mind" I smiled at her and tried to calm her, "she needs to rest" Her mother just nodded and showed me the way, the tears not stopping. I lay Aurelia on her bed and brushed the wisps of her out of her face behind her ear. I turn to her mother who was watching me carefully "I will go now"

Hey guys, I hope that you enjoyed all the chapters. Thanks for your votes and comments. And I'm sorry for not posting this week, it was just stressful for me.

But I'm posting another chapter this weekend.

Love, moon.

05

Aurelia Moreno

I woke up to a loud argument. I groaned to myself "who would be argue this loud in the morning?" But then I heard my Mom, how she shouts at my Dad and she was crying. I could hear her sobbing from here. I was furios at the person who made my mother cry and was ready to eat the shit out of them. So I got up and dressed myself.

As I looked at myself in the mirror of my bathroom, the events of the night came straight back into my head. Vomit formed it self in my mouth and I was eager to get over the toilet and throw up. I felt disgusted by myself and just wanted to delete all those memories.

I made my way down the stairs to the living room. The first thing I saw were pillows from the sofas laying everywhere. I thing this was my Mother, but they weren't here. I think they were in the kitchen, so I made my way. I saw my Mother snapping at my father, her whole head was red from anger. Mom stood at the one side of the kitchen island with her back towards me and my Dad stood on the other, directly looking at me.

"You can't just do that to our girl, she's not even an adult. You are not in you right mind." she shouted, Dad tried to calm her.

"Carolina-" he tried but was cut off by Mom, who was a crying mess. I decided to stay quiet and to not taking any attention to me.

"No you are going to listen to me now!" she snapped at him. Dad just now noticed my presence.

"Morning Aurelia" Dad said, hinting Mom to stop talking. What are they hiding?

"Morning Dad" I smiled at him and went towards Mom, "Morning Ma'" I said kissing her on the cheeks ,smiling.

"Morning Honey, are you hungry? I could make you some breakfast the cook isn't here today." She tried to get away from the argument they had earlier.

"Uhm yes" I shrug "Could you make just some cereal?" I asked, I wasn't that hungry the events from yesterday still in my head making vomit form in my mouth and me wanting to throw up again. But I still wanted to comfort her and to not make her anxious.

"Yes of course, nothing else? I could make you a fruit plate, you like them so much" she asked, hopeful that I would want more. I nodded and she went straight to work. I looked at my Dad while Mom was in the pantry looking for the things she will need.

"What was that about?" I asked, trying to know about what they've talked or more argued. I wanted to know it before Mom would be back making my breakfast. The tension in the room was thick and my Dad was clearly uncomfortable in the state I've brought him in. I look at him with concern till he finally answers.

"Oh you know nothing what is about your concern" he tried to ease the tension in the room. You know Mom and I could just look at him with this one look and he would tell us instantly. I think I've inherited the look from my Mother, she would do it constantly and Dad would give in and tell her.

"We will go to Italy tomorrow, because of an important meeting with the De Luca's. And the Mafia ball will be there this year too." Dad said, I scuff, that was not it. Mom came into the kitchen again with my Breakfast. She eagerly motioned for me to sit down on one of the kitchen island stools.

"Here you go Honey, eat up we have to do some shopping." she smiled at me and put the plates in front of me. Of course she had made more food that I've requested. And she knows that I hate to throw food away that still could have been eaten.

"Thank you Mom" I smile at her, "You go get ready I'll finish and then we can meet up at the door" I make her known that she is still in her pj's. She agreed and went upstairs to get ready. "Here Dad take something, you know that I can't eat all that.." I say pointing at the food in front of me as soon as Mom was out of sight. Dad laughs and sits next to me and starts to take himself a plate.

-

"Sweetie let's go, we need to buy you a dress for the Ball." Mom said to me as she looked at me so I would hurry up. "Bye Leo" Mom shouted at the top of her lungs to get my Fathers attention. And she did he came going fast down the stairs.

"You are going to take bodyguards with you." Dad said sternly and called some bodyguards. Mom wanted to refuse but Dad cut her off, "Have you forgotten Carolina?" he asked, Mom shook her head.

"No in fact I didn't but can't we have some that are in the background endnote present all the time?" Mom asked sternly, father nodded his head and soon five bodyguards step out of the elevator.

"You will have five bodyguards with you, they'll be more background and you won't even notice them." Dad said pointing to the five man in front of us. "And then we have her," he pointed at a woman that I didn't even see at first, "This is Eloise, she will be more present but will let you do your thing." I was actually pretty relieved that we had someone around all the time. "Have fun and don't buy too much money." Dad said pointing at my Mother as he said the last part. I couldn't restrain myself from laughing, though only a soft one.

"Thank you, and-" Mom was cut off by my father, who gave her a kiss on the lips. "Cora I have to go. In fact I'm in the middle of a meeting right now and the boys won't want to wait so long" He smiled at her, "Go have fun and buy our daughter a beautiful dress and maybe even yourself something." He smiled and gave her his card "Love you" He says and walked back upstairs.

My Mom looked after him dumbfounded, "Love you too, and I don't need your credit card Idiot" she called after him, and I swear to God I could hear him chuckle.

"Mom come on." I urge her to get into the elevator.

-

Currently we were in the fifth boutique and my Mother still couldn't decide which dress I should wear. Don't think that I haven't found one, I have already shown her countless dresses and even put them on, but she is still not satisfied. I had a beautiful velvet green silk dress on, which hugged my body perfectly. It had a slit on one side, the streps were thin and had to be knotted. The dress was a bit longer than ankle long but if I would wear heels then it wouldn't be a problem.

"I think that's the one" I said to my Mom, who was still rummaging through the other dresses. I wait for to look at me, but of course she didn't hear me. Ugh I hate it when your parents won't stay seated in front of your changing room. Like my Mom never stays there and walks through half of the store. "Mom?!" I call a bit louder and that catches her attention and she finally looks at me, "I think that's the one" I repeat.

She nods and says "I think that's the one too. But you will probably need another one or maybe even two." she says and grabs another dress. It was golden and looked a bit alike the other one, I currently have on. The dress was shorter, but not too much, it was just up to the knees. The rest was simply the same as the green one, but it looked a bit cuter. Mom saw my reaction and gave it to me, "Go try it on." she ushered me into the changing room.

I put it on and look into the mirror. I imagined it with the right make up and jewelry it looked so gorgeous, though I know it won't in real live. I take a step out of the changing room and saw my Mothers eyes light up. "I kinda want to have it." I smile at her.

"Darling, we are buying it. Don't care if you want it or not. I will simply force you to wear it." she smiled and took the green dress from me, "And I even have another one" she held up a white dress which was floor length, it wasn't bad but it looked like I would get married.

"Mom this looks like I would get married." I shake my head and refuse to try it on. But she had other thoughts instead of not forcing me she gave me the dress into my hand and closed the curtains. I groan to myself and change. I looked in the mirror and indeed looked like I was getting married. I step out and look at my mom, "I look like I'm marrying some dude." I state.

"Now stand up right, and I think it looks cute. Don't you think Eloise?" Mom asked her, she looked at us dumbfounded. Eloise clearly hadn't listen to our conversation ,which I love. "I asked if she didn't looked cute in this dress?" Mom smiled at her and she smiled.

"I think she looks as if she is going to marry someone, don't get me wrong it looks cute." she scrunched up her nose and looked me up and down.

"See mom" I say and get changed back. This is going to be a long fucking day.

06

Aurelia Moreno

It's the next day and I have just finished packing my things for the next week. Right now I'm getting ready for the flight there. Dad said we would leave in approximately one hour, so I still have a lot of time. I went downstairs for breakfast after doing my hair and makeup. I wore something simple, comfortable yet not looking lazy.

"Morning" I called to our chef cook, who was occupied by cooking some bacon and eggs. "Can you make me some of these too?" I asked getting myself some orange juice and a glass. I looked inside the dining room and could see my Mother on her phone playing some game while drinking her morning tea, her hair is still wrapped in a towel. Dad iss no where to be seen.

"Oh haven't seen you there, of course Aurelia it will be ready in some minutes" she said glancing at the clock. I nod at her and walk into the dining room, Mom's head snaps up and she smiles at me.

"Morning Honey. How have you slept?" she asked putting her phone down. "I have slept good." I answer and sit on the chair opposites of hers. We talked for a bit more and were interrupted by the cook who brought our food to us. We both thanked her and started eating, it tasted so good.

-

I knock on his Office door and open the door. There he sits his mug with coffee in his hands and typing away on his laptop. "Hey Dad, I wanted to ask if you were ready. We are waiting for you" I say. He looks up at me and then down at his laptop again.

"Yes Honey, we will leave in twenty minutes." I nodded and was about to go out of the room when he stops me, "Oh and Aurelia ask your Mom if she could pack my bag. I didn't get around to it." He smiles at me. Oh no if my Mom would know that she has to pack his bag in twenty minutes.

"You haven't packed your bag?" I asked astonished, "You know Mom-" I was cut off by him.

"Yes I know your Mom and please don't even make it worse, just try to ask her as fast as you can so she isn't that angry with me." he rubbed his temples.

"Right I'm going to tell her." I said closing the door behind me and running down the stairs as fast as I could. "Mom!" I call out for her and find her sitting on one of the sofas, reading some magazine. "Mom." I say out of breath, she turns towards me and raises an eyebrow at me, "Dad asked if you could pack his bag for him he hadn't had the time for it.." I try to tell her the nicest way possibly, I didn't want a Mom who was angry at me.

"Oh that fucker, he will-" she curses under her breath and stands up, I hold her from running upstairs, "Hey calm down, he probably had his reasons why he couldn't" Although I know that he was just to lazy for it, I tried to calm her down. "You are right, I'm gonna pack his bag." she smiles at me and heads upstairs.

-

I took a step out of the jet. Letting the fresh Italian breeze welcome me.

Finally in Italy, I love it here. We got into a car which was send to take us to the De Luca estate. Their estate was way bigger than ours. The fact that I've been here half of my childhood brought many memories back. At that Tree I've captivates Mr. Romano with the help of Sofia, the sister of Luciano and one of my best friends, we were bored since we had an Spanish lesson and couldn't figure out anything more fun than captivating our teacher.

Or that lake there, me and Sofia used to take one of the boats and row on the lake till one of the bodyguards had to safe us because our parents thought it was too unsafe for us. We weren't even in the need of help to come back, but we thought it was funny how the bodyguard tried to safe us either they swam or took a boat.

Or the flower field there, with a beautiful view at the ocean. Me and Sofia would sneak out and play in the big garden and after some time our mothers got worried so again they send bodyguards to look for us. And when they found us and told us what could have happened we would run to the flower field get some flowers and give them our moms as a sorry. Then we would always ramble about how sorry we are till our moms hugged us so we shut up and then we would eat ice cream together.

The car took a hold and my parents got out. I went out after them and first thing I did was taking a deep breath of the ocean air.

"AURELIA" someone screamed, and that someone was Sofia. God I missed her so much. I ran towards her "Aurelia, finally you're here I have so much to tell you" I hugged her and she hugged me back "I've missed you so much" "Me too" we let go of each other and she took me inside the castle.

"I have so fucking much to tell you. We haven't seen each other in so long-" and then she rambled on about thinks that happened the last time that I have seen her. I have fucking missed her, she is one of my best friends to be honest my only one. I don't have many friends because I don't know many people. I was home schooled never have seen a Kindergarden from inside and never had a hobby which I couldn't do at home. Dad was overprotective and didn't want anyone to know about me for my safety, but I think that's because of a different reason.

Which was 13 years ago. Yeah 13 years of things that she did. Well of course not everything but some interesting stuff like that she got to go to Canada whens she was 15. That was the first time that she actually went into a French speaking country. I was never in a French speaking country although my Mom is half French, she never took me there.

-

"Girls come on dinner" Mom and Victoria called "Ok were coming" Sofia said as response and made our way down to the dining hall. We have been in her room since we have arrived and talked about just our lives. We walk down the big corridors and then down the big pair of stairs. I remember the time Sofia and I used the stair railing as a slide and then I broke my arm.

"You can sit next to me." I smiled at her and sat next to her. Everyone was already seated. My Mother sat next to my Father opposite to me and Sofia, Luciano was seated next to Dad. And on the heads off the table sat Victoria and Lorenzo. Soon the chef cook brought the food and placed the plates in front of us.

I looked at the dish curious, I have never eaten anything like that it looked like a soup with some sort of vegetables. "It's Minestrone, it is made up of different kinds of seasonal chopped vegetables often paired with potatoes, beans and Mushrooms. Sometimes it's even served with little pasta. It is a healthy and light recipe try it" Luciano encourages me to try it, which I did.

It didn't taste like a soup I would eat back at the states it had more spice in it, honestly the best soup I've ever had in my Life.

"It's good" I say pointing at the soup looking at Luciano, who chuckles lightly. I eat the whole plate of soup and wait for the next dish excitely. And soon enough there was the cook again, some of his helpers took the dirty plates with them and he served the next dish. To my disappointment it was something with seafood. And I hate seafood, I could eat fish now and then but if it comes to mussels then I'm gonna pass.

I ate some of the Focaccia, which is a flat leavened oven-baked Italian bread, similar in style and texture to pizza. And I love it, I could've only eating this for the entire day and would be perfectly happy. And then the cook brought the last dish before the dessert. Which was of course pasta with a home made tomato sauce or seafood sauce, of course I chose the tomato one.

I think homemade pasta plus sauce is the best you could ever eat in you life. I really love it and I hope I can make my own ones soon too. And soon dessert was brought, they made Tiramisu, which is one of my favorites. Basically it's a coffee-flavoured Italian dessert. It is made of ladyfingers dipped in coffee, layered with a whipped mixture of eggs, sugar, and mascarpone cheese, flavored with cocoa.

We talked briefly as we ate making the whole dinner take two hours. "Hey sweetie we wanted to talk to you after dinner, could you come to our room then?" Mom asked while eating seafood, I just nod and get back to my conversation with Sofia. We talked about some type of animal which had a big ass nose and mouth is mostly colored in a light shade of pink. I don't even know how we came to this conversation.

After eating and kinda moving in my room, which only considered of unpacking half of the clothing I took with me, I went to my parents room and knocked lightly. "Come in" moms voice said, so I opened the door and went inside.

"Hey sweetie" Mom said, smiling at me. She motioned for me to the other side of the room "Hey mom" I walk over and see my Dad sitting on a chair typing away on his laptop.

"Aurelia, Honey sit down" Dad said not even looking up from his laptop, rude much. I went over and sat down. "So.." he finally looked up at me and smiled, "let's start this conversation. Where do I begin. You know Luciano is the hier to the Italian Mafia Empire," I nod in response, "Well our fathers actually made a deal. They said that their grandchildren will marry each other so that the alliance between our two Mafias will be stronger than ever before. And because you guys are old enough and are both legal to marry. We want you guys to-" I cut him off by mumbling "to marry each other"

I start to laugh, they can't be serious right now Grandpa always loved me, he wouldn't have done such a deal in his life. This had to be a big joke, where are the cameras? "So you guys want us to marry just so your guises stupid alliance is stronger? Are you in your fucking right mind? Grandpa would have never done such thing."

Dad just shook his head, "No Aurelia I'm serious, you are gonna marry Luciano. And you will sign a contract where everything will be explained more." he stated at me anger flooding right through his body, "And I will not repeat myself"

I looked at him with shocked eyes. This can't be happening right now. They always told me that I could get my own partner and then thing about marry them not like this. Is my Life a fucking joke? Who do they thing they are? Jesus?

"I think I need fresh air" I say as I walk out of the room slowly.

"Someone go with her" my dad said and a bodyguard followed me outside.

07

Aurelia Moreno

I looked at him with shocked eyes. This can't be happening right now. They always told me that I could get my own partner and then thing about marry them not like this. Is my Life a fucking joke? Who do they thing they are? Jesus?

"I think I need fresh air" I say as I walk out of the room slowly.

"Someone go with her" my dad said and a bodyguard followed me outside.

I walked down the long corridors towards the backyards with a beautiful view of the ocean and city. I loved it there as a kid and it reminded me of home and hope. Mother would always read stories for me and Sofia in this backyards and Victoria would bring some snacks for us, later our Dads would join after they worked. And it would look just like as if we were two completely normal families.

I couldn't do it. I couldn't marry someone right now. Someone I hate, someone who doesn't even know me. Someone who hates me as much as I hate him. Someone I couldn't think a future with.

I looked behind me. Seeing the bodyguard following me every step didn't please me. I wanted to run away, but he would reach and catch me. So I made myself a plan. Just as he was looking somewhere else to give me privacy, I take a run. I run fast.

Behind me I can hear "wait Aurelia" being yelled. I look behind me and see that he is too far behind me to reach me and that's when I bumped into something or someone. I fall to the floor and get up quickly. In front of me lays a boy, more specific Luciano. I quickly help him up and say my sorry's.

"Oh my gosh I'm so sorry" I say while extending my hand for him to grab. He does and soon he is standing on his two feet again.

"It's ok" He says while dusting off his pants, "Why are you running anyways?" he asks slightly looking up at me. I try to find a lie that was getting me out of this situation. But then I saw the Bodyguard again, how he run towards us and this time he had some more Men with him. Are you kidding me? I gotta go,

"well I have to get going" I say as I run again , well that was weird I think to myself. I see him looking after me with a weird look, I just shake my head and run faster to get away from them.

Luciano

I watch as she runs her way out of the estate backyard. Aurelia runs pretty fast I have to say, but why is she running anyways? As if she is running from someone who is going to kill her. MY thoughts were cut short by some De Luca bodyguards and one of my under sotto-capo who is underboss for France.

"I'm sorry Boss, but have you seen Aurelia Moreno running?" Henri asks, clearly out of breath.

"Yes I indeed have, she has run this way. You wanna be fast she is a pretty good runner." I chuckle. What has she done so that she has to run this fast and from so many people? And why are they out of breath, she doesn't even run that fast.

"Thank you Luciano." Henri says and starts running again. I'm interested in the thing she has done again. And I have to restrain myself from running with them. But now I have to go to mom and dad they wanted to talk to me.

Aurelia

I was running and because I saw no-one behind me and I felt exhausted, I made a little break at a tree. Ok not exactly at a tree I would more say on a tree so they couldn't really see me if they would ran past here. So I climbed up and watched the beautiful sunset. It was so peaceful. I could hear the birds chirping and the wind as it blows.

"There she is" that didn't go to plan, I looked down in shook and saw more bodyguards standing down there, pointing at me. Now there is no way out of here. So I'll just stay up here.

"Miss Moreno please come down from there" one pleaded. I don't know but he didn't look like any of these Bodyguards down there, he looked as if he is a higher 'level'.

"Miss Aurelia please" they could stay down there as long as they want, I'm NOT coming down there. And anyway it's so beautiful up here. "Miss Moreno what would your dad say right now if he could see you sitting up there?" Oh no not my Dad, I'm gonna be in so much trouble. If he would know. He would describe me as a childish kid or something like this.

"No worries I'm gonna come down." I said climbing down. As my feet touch the ground a Man came to me and checked if I was ok "I'm ok no worries" I say holding my hands up.

"Thank god, this could've turned out bad" he said as he checked my face "Anyways I'm Henri, one of Lucianos sotto-capos. It's my pleasure to finally meet you, Sofia told me a lot about you." he smiled and motioned for me to walk in the direction of the mansion. I hope this bitch only said good things about me because this situation is not gonna give a good first impression.

We walk back towards the mansion in silent the only thing heard is our feet touching the gravel. Opening the door to my bedroom Henri, the only one who was following me, said that he will not tell my Dad and neither will one of the bodyguards. I was thankful for that because if my Dad knew what I had tried he would be real mad and Mom probably too.

I got ready for bed and looked out the window. The sun was still setting and I could see the ocean clearly. There were little boats everywhere. I went to bed really exhausted of the journey from Portugal to Italy.

08

A urelia Moreno

I woke up to the birds chirping outside and the sun creeping through the curtain. I open my eyes looking around. First I went to the bathroom and after that to the window. I could see the waves of the ocean, the beautiful flower field with kids playing catch. I saw some employees doing their work, maintaining the Garden. I catch a glimpse of a black Lamborghini driving down the drive way and parking in one of the garages. But then I had put my focus back on nature.

Today was going to be a stressful day, the ball is coming and I was a bit nervous. Though not that exited to be honest. I just want to get this over with.

I got ready and put on some comfy clothes. After that I went to the dining hall, Sofia was already there eating breakfast.

"Morning Sof" I mumble and sat down next to her after asking the cook to do my breakfast of course.. We were the only ones currently sitting here and eating breakfast. The others were probably planning the Ball.

"Good morning" she smiled, "Today is the Ball are you excited."

"Miss your breakfast" Some kitchen employee said and gave me my plate with scrambled eggs and pancakes. Soon Victoria came inside with her husband and son. They all sat down and began to make conversations with us, except for Luciano who was occupied on his phone typing away. Probably to someone who is important to him.

After I was finished I stood up and wanted to go to my room to get ready. but was stopped by Mom who called out for me. "Remember Aurelia the ball is going to start at 8pm" my mother said, "Be ready." she called after me.

"Yep" I say making my way to my room.

-

Later that day I got ready for the ball. I wore the velvet silk green satin dress, with some silver heels. My Makeup was pretty, my lips were colored in a light pink shade I had some highlighter on and of course some mascara. That was basically it. Oh and don't forget my Jewelry. I wore a golden necklace which Mom and Dad got me for my 18th Birthday, I haven't put it down once. Aside from that I wore some adorable, little not so chunky earrings and an elegant bracelet.

A knock on the door startled me. "Aurelia you there?" a voice ,that I think Sofia was, asked me. I wasn't finished yet, I still had to put the shoes on but still welcomed her in.

"Yea come in" I said and soon I'm face to face with Sofia "Oh my gosh you look so beautiful". She wore a beautiful cream dress with rhinestones around the neck of the dress. Her necklace were matching with the earrings, who were silver looking with a tiny glamorous gemstone.

"Look at you" she pointed at my dress with an 'o' shaped mouth "This so beautiful, remember me that you have to tell me were you bought it." I smile at her and put the heels on.

"I bought it with my Mom in a boutique in New York, you definitely have to visited some time. We could go shopping and I could show you the shop." I smiled at her, and she nodded her head.

"Hey girls it's time." my Mother came in my room "You are already late, we are all waiting for you." she smiled. Mom looked breathtaking she had on a beige dress, the sleeves go to her elbow and the dress goes till her ankles. She wore the jewelry Dad got her when they married and the one necklace I bought her for Mothers day when I was 12. I didn't bought it alone Dad helped me.

We all walked together to the big Ball room. Dad stood in front of the door smiling at us "You guys are so beautiful, but we have to go inside." he pointed at the big door. I could hear the music playing inside and many people talking. I have often been at such events but never have I been here in Italy for the Mafia Ball.

When we were here and this ball would be celebrated, me and Sofia would stay in one of the playrooms all night and some nanny would look after us. Apparently our parents thought it was too dangerous for us to be down here.

"Come on Chérie. - Darling." Mom said clinging herself with my Dad's arm. Mom and Dad went first and then Sofia and I followed them.

The first thing that I noticed when we went inside was some people, well women, staring at me with their beautiful dresses, or suits, I saw some women with suits on earlier. I don't like it when people stare at me, I think it's kind of rude to make people so uncomfortable.

But I like giraffes. You know I have never seen giraffes in real life but in pictures. And let me tell you, they look so cute. Thats what I wanna do later when I'm old, or not, I wanna go on safari and look at giraffes in real life.

Anyways back to real life. Me and Sofia firstly walked towards the drinks. We took us some punch and walked towards a sitting area were many people were seated and talked about I think business.

"You look so beautiful, you know, you will probably find your price charming today here in this ballroom." she smiled imagining what we have dreamed about for years. Oh hell if she knew.

"I don't know. Anyways I'm just twenty years old, I have time." I state and look at her, "And I think that you will find your boy earlier than I do, I mean look at you all the boys were drooling at you."

She blushed a bit and turned her head slightly. This Bitch what is she hiding. "You know, I have met somebody," Ohhhhh, now I'm curious. "His name is Dante. He is one of Lucianos sotto-capo. - underboss." she smiled at me, and blushes slightly.

"Does Luciano know?" I've been cut short.

"No he doesn't and if he would, then Dante wouldn't really be alive anymore. Please don't talk about this conversation with anyone. Okay?" I just nod my head. As if this Chienne {- Bitch} would ever kill an underboss from him.

We talked for a bit more before until it was time to dance. I didn't feel like dancing.

"You wanna share this dance with me?" a beautiful voice said. I turned around just to find a charming boy standing in front of me.

"it would be my pleasure" I smiled at him, I had to. My dad was watching me, next to him was Luciano talking to my Father about what I think is business, again. Luciano watched me intensely, watching every move I made. He clenched his jaw as he saw that the boy took my hand. He pretends as if I'm his.

"Whats your name if I can ask" He asked softly as he led me to the dance floor.

"Oh I'm sorry, my name is Aurelia" Why would he ask a person to dance that he didn't even knew. I mean how dumb can you be. Anyway i'ts not as if he's bad looking. We stood more in the middle of the dance floor and he begins to lead the dance.

"Well nice meeting you Aurelia, I'm Antonio" he smiled, we danced always further outwards the center more to the right. We stood right next to a window. The stars looking really beautiful, shining in their glory.

He was a pretty good dancer. Now I haven't danced with many people, just 3, anyways but the first boy I've ever danced with stepped on my foot all the time, the second one couldn't take all the spins so he went to throw up in the bathroom after just 5 min. And this Antonio guy is my third time dancing on a ball, other than my dad.

I was startled out of my thoughts by someone forcing Antonio of of me. I looked at him as he stared back at me. Of course it has to be Luciano, what was he thinking?

"Bro what's up, haven't seen you in a while" Antonio asked, Luciano talked with him but only looked at me, and I looked back in shock. How can he scare me so much?

Luciano glared at me. Why would he glare at me? I did nothing wrong.

"I'm good, how are you?" Luciano asks, "I think you have met Aurelia," He pointed at me. Antonio nodded, "Anyways I was eagerly to talk to you about business." He and Antonio turned around walking away, slowly towards the sitting area. "How is business in Spain with Dante, I heard that he found Love?" was the last thing I heard from them.

09

A urelia Moreno

"I'm good, how are you?" Luciano asks, "I think you have met Aurelia," He pointed at me. Antonio nodded, "Anyways I was eagerly to talk to you about business." He and Antonio turned around walking away, slowly towards the sitting area. "How is business in Spain with Dante, I heard that he found Love?" was the last thing I heard from them.

I walked out of the ball room. Luckily nobody saw what was going on and nobody saw me going out of the room. I went to the graden again and sat down at a bench watching the sky full of stars.

Somebody cleared their throat behind me. I turned around and saw that it was him again. I didn't want to talk to this fucker right now. I mean, How bold can you be? I was just dancing getting to know some new people.

Luciano took my arm so that I had to look at him. I winced in pain, why does this fucker have to grab this harsh as if I'm going to run any minute. To be honest I wanted to do that so bad. I would do anything so I don't have to look at him. "You know the next time you want to dance don't choose one of the-" he was cut off by someone clearing their throat.

"Ah you guys, we were actually searching for you" my father said, making me look at him questioningly, what the fuck does he want? First Luciano and now Dad?

"We wanted to talk to you guys but then you guys just disappeared" Lorenzo chuckled, who I hadn't noticed. He stood now beside my Dad smiling at us. Luciano let my arm go and looked at his father. "Okay guys come on inside we have some things to talk about and it's cold here." He said and both my Father and Lorenzo walked towards the building.

Luciano firstly stared at them but then made his way towards the building. I stared at them some time, till they turned around and waited for me.All of them stared at me for some time till I followed them too.

We were in Lorenzos office "please sit down we have to talk about so many things" he smiled glancing at me. I smiled back and sat down, he and my father did the same only Luciano stood aside watching his Dad. "Ok so you guys know that you'll be marrying each other in some months, we don't actually know how many we still have to think about it. We'll give you a week for you guys to get to know each other, nothing more." he stated.

A week. A fucking week. Are you kidding me? Why so freaking fast?

"A fucking week?" Luciano said, staring at his father perplex. That's the same I thought! Soulmates, kidding.

"Yes Luciano, one week nothing more! We are running out of time." his father said, Luciano sighed angry and went out of the door but not shutting it normally no, he had to slam the door.

Lorenzo sighed "Ok so we have to do this with out him" he gave me a paper "Luciano already signed it so now you have to sign it Aurelia."

"And what if I won't sign it what will you do?" I asked, looking up.

"Then this will be a forced marriage" Lorenzo and my Dad said at the same time, creepy. Anyway this is a forced marriage so. And to make it not more difficult I signed it. I fucking signed it. Of course I've read all the stuff on the piece of paper before signing it. My mom taught me this, she would be proud. Hopefully.

Now you ask what is written on this piece of paper, well we have to marry. And that's all and do stuff what married couples do like share a house and stuff like that. There is no where written that we have to share a bed with is comforting.

"So since this contract is signed and both of them have agreed to marry, we can finally start with the preparations." my Dad smiled "Your Mom will be so proud of you, her only child marrying"

"And Victorias only son" Lorenzo smiled. I just felt a bit creeped out. Only a tiny bit.

"Okay so may I go now, since everything is done" I asked, trying to sound as polite as ever.

"Yes you can go now" Lorenzo said.

I slip out of the room and found Luciano prepped against the wall looking at me, or the door but you know we are at the same place right now. "Have you signed it?" he sighed. Why is he sighing now?

"Yes?" I said or more asked. He had signed it too.

"I had hoped you wouldn't." He sighed again, "But I'm proven wrong, again." He mumbled the last part. "Are you in your fucking right mind? You have to marry me you know that, right?" He basically screamed at me. I winced back a bit startled by the situation.

"Luciano I had no other choice. We would have married anyway, even if we didn't sign the contract." I shouted back. He just chuckled. Why would he chuckle in such a moment? I'm done. I walked towards the stairs, I just wanted to go into my room and to bed. Nothing more. But was stopped by someone grabbing my arm and pulling me back.

I was hurled back into a chest. Lucianos to be more accurate. He spun me around and pressed me against a wall. His face was getting closer and my breathing increased. What is he doing? I felt his breathe brush against my neck and his hands finding their way to my waist, holding me steady.

And then he stopped. He quickly stepped back and looked at me cursing under his breath. I only saw his figure running up the stairs.

Hi guys. guess who might got the covid, anyways. Thank you for 100 reads, the book is nearly done and I can't wait that you guys can all read the whole book.

10

- -

A urelia Moreno

And then he stopped. He quickly stepped back and looked at me cursing under his breath. I only saw his figure running up the stairs.

What was his problem. I just stood there looking into the void. After some time I decided to go back into the ballroom. Sofia most likely was looking for me. I don't fucking know how to tell her. And when should I even tell her? I mean I just can't go to her and say 'oh and by the way I marrying your brother. But not as in love as in an arranged marriage.'

I got into the ballroom and went straight to Sofia. "Hey were where you?" she asked watching as the people on the dance floor.

"Just outside watching stars and such, enjoying the fresh summer air" I smiled.

"Oh yeah I love watching the stars at late summer nights" she smiled back "You know we have to do something like this, maybe this week" she looked up at the ceiling "For how long are you staying, we have to plan everything" she looked at me, uh how long am I staying and how am I gonna tell her about this thing with her brother. But she will probably see this as a good thing, we wanted to be sisters for so long, and now we will finally be. But that's not the right moment to tell her, hell I'm not even realizing it.

"Uhm I would say for some months surely" I smiled

"Okay so we have plenty of time and plenty of things to do" she smiled back "What do you think we can do?" Oh I have thought so many times about this, what I wanna do with my best friend in the near future or late future doesn't really care.

I wanna go to New York or Los Angeles. I wanna see the polar lights and go to china. I wanna go to China so bad, the food, the culture, the people, everything. China is literally something I wanna do so bad and of course safari, finally being able to see giraffes in real life and of course zebras, elephants, lions and other animals. But giraffes. What else do I wanna do?

Explore Italy. Not big cities in Italy more like little ones or even villages. I heard that some of them are quite beautiful. And then I want to eat pizza at a little restaurant with a beautiful view over what ever we are.

I wanna go to England, having somewhat bad weather for a week or something like this and exploring London. Eating an English breakfast with eggs and stuff like this and baked beans never had them before.

Germany, I wanna go to Germany and eat the food there. Did you know that they eat raw meat? Well I did. I wanna see these people with dirndls and their beer (ok that might be reproachful because I don't think that they were it every day).

I wanna go to Brazil and see these cool beaches that everyone is talking about.

Some people told me that New Zealand is quite interesting too, they have beautiful nature, but now let's be honest I don't wanna see nature all the time. And I was in New Zealand before, when I was 5 but don't care. It was 15 years ago, I don't remember a thing.

"I wanna go swimming in the ocean with dolphins or something like this" Sofia said. Oh no I'm not gonna go into the ocean, I hate it when I don't know what's under me or swims with me. And have you see Wales, no they are so big I can't swim.

"No, we could go on safari seeing other wild animals but I will not swim with dolphins in the ocean" I tried to talk her out of it.

"Why not?" she asked, I sighed.

"You don't really know what's bellow you" I said

"Yeah you're right but-" she was cut of by a bang. Everyone in the room screams and runs to get out of the room. People are shot and fall to the ground, I look around to find my mom and dad when someone throws me and the ground and get on top of me.

"Go away" I scream, you can't really hear me because of the other people screaming I look up to seeing Luciano shielding me with his body "What are you doing Luciano?" I asked him, while staring at him with wide eyes.

"What does it look like? I'm trying to help you, so you won't get shot" Dumbass, of course I know that he's trying that I won't die, but why is he doing it? I look around, people are running and trying to get somewhere safe. Some don't make it and fall to the ground, lifeless. I hear children crying and calling for their parents and I could see men coming into the room with guns trying to shoot every person in the room.

I could see Luciano taking out a gun, out of his pants, and pointing it at men, shooting them.

"Okay so here is the plan we will get up and run to this door there" he pointed at a door that was farthest away "Then you are going to go up the stairs" I nod "and go to the last door, go inside close and lock the door" I nod again "Okay we are gonna go when I say go" he says while he is getting of of me so I can run.

"Go" he said and takes my hand. Both of us ran as fast as we could and soon we were out of the room and in a hallway, he closes the door behind us and I let out a breath that I didn't know I was holding. We stayed with our back against the door for some seconds just breathing before I glanced down at my shoes.

I saw that we were still holding hands, I let go as fast as I could. He looked down at his handed looks up at me "Ok so now go upstairs and do what I told you, I will get you when it's safe okay?" I just nod " Okay go" I run as fast as I could in my dress and these shoes, which aren't perfect for running, and went the stairs into the last room. I closed the door behind me. After I've heard the click sound ,signaling me that the door was locked, I turned around and looked around the room.

The first thing I saw was a bed. A big bed, the room was decorated in darker colors. I saw an office desk with a laptop and two doors. I opened the first one just to see a big bathroom. After looking around the bathroom, which was more white and gray, I went out of it and opened the next door which showed a big closed with many clothes. But they didn't fill the whole room. It was just the half, the other half was free. I liked the room. It was modern but not to modern.

I went into the main room again and went to a big window ,that I didn't notice before because it was dark outside. I looked out and saw the beautiful backyard with it's flowers. It could have been such a beautiful peace moment.

But I could hear the screams of people down stairs and thought about Mom and Dad and where they could've went for safety. I thought about where Sofia went, she was next to me the exact moment maybe Luciano took care of her and brought here somewhere safe. Somewhere where she wouldn't be found by these people.

I sat down on the bed and look at the room decor a bit before falling asleep. The last sound I heard was like a door opening and then closing again.

11

A urelia Moreno

I woke up and looked around.Where am I? Then all the events of yesterday came back. I'm still in the same room. But this time under a blanket. And my shoes are of, I look under the blanket and see that I'm not wearing my dress anymore.

Just my underwear. Okay everything is okay, I have my underwear on. No panic I have my... my

FUCKING UNDERWEAR ON?

Who the fuck-? and why? and when?

Why am I only wearing my Underwear? In a room which I don't even know?

I looked around some more and saw someone sleeping on the couch in the room. I got up and went to check who it was, when I accidentally bumped a lamp on the bedside table. It fell and rattled on the floor. It broke. Fuck.

The person jumped up and looked at me first, it was Luciano. I sheepish smiled at him. He got up and went to crouch in front of me. "Are you okay?" he asked which took me by shock.

"Uhm yea" I nodded and went to grab the broken glass to throw it away.

"Wait, you'll cut yourself" he stoped me and took the broken glass and threw it away himself. Uhm okay? Who is this person and what did they do to Luciano?

"Who is this? And what did you do to Luciano?" I said staring at him, he chuckled.

"I'm me" he said, I narrowed my eyes at him. I got up and forgot for a slight second that I just wore basically nothing. I quickly grabbed the blanket and threw it around myself. Luciano chuckled and grabbed some tissues, which apparently where next to the bed? I don't even want to know who's room this is or was and why they have tissues next to their bed?

Why is he even in this room, couldn't he go to his own? And why would he sent me up here, I could've just went to my room and everything would be perfectly fine.

"Why are you even here" I asked, he was now sitting besides me.

"This is my room Aurelia, why shouldn't I be here" Oh

"Anyway" he chuckled again "did anyone got hurt?" I asked hoping nobody got hurt.

"Well" he stumbled over his words, oh no, I looked at him in shock. He saw the fear in my eyes and went over to his playful side "nobody, only some guests but I guess you haven't asked if they got hurt, haven't you?" he chuckled, dumbass.

"You asshole" I took the first thing next to me, it was a pillow, and hit him on the head. If I think about it now, if wanted to hurt him, I should've took something different, like the other lamp or a book.

"Did you think this would hurt?" he chuckled, and grabbed the pillow so I would stop hitting him.

"No I didn't" I said getting up to leave the room, I tightened the blanket around myself so it wouldn't fall down while I walked. I opened the door and before I went out, I flipped him off. Now he sat there his mouth wide open, staring at me in disbelief.

I slammed the door shut and went to my room, which was sadly only 2 doors next to his. But better than nothing.

I went inside and locked the door behind me. I didn't want any unnecessary attention, so I went into the bed and turned a bit so it looked like that I went to bed here yesterday. After this I opened the windows and closed the curtains, I would sleep like that every night. Then I went to my bathroom and brushed my teeth, took my smeared make up off and took a quick shower.

After the shower, which was really refreshing, I went into the closed and took out some clothes. Not a dress or something like this and went back into the bathroom. After I got ready I heard a knock on my door.

"Honey, are you awake already?" my mothers voice asked "Yes mom I'm in the bathroom" I called back.

"Okay after you're done can you come into Lorenzos office?" uh not again "Uhm of course, just give me some minutes" I said confused. Why would they want to have me there again, wasn't yesterday enough?

After some minutes pacing in the bathroom, about what could've happen or about what would happen, I finally went to the office.

I knocked on the door and after I heard a 'come in' I went inside.

"Aurelia sweetie why don't you sit down?" Victoria said smiling, I sat down next to Luciano. Which apparently was the only seat left, sadly. I could have also stood all the time, that would have been no problem for me.

"Guys I know it's hard for you guys to do this, but we have found a date when we will do the wedding" Lorenzo said. My eyes widen.

"It's in 2 weeks, we don't have so much time to move it further back" my Dad said looking at us both.

"Luciano, you will propose to Aurelia in 3 days" Victoria said looking at a stunned Luciano.

"We will do a ball for this sake in some days. After you proposed to her." Lorenzo said looking at Luciano too. "The rings will be exchanged there." My eyes even widen more, if it could even work. Couldn't we do it in private with out so many people, and what I even say to Sofia. She would see all this. "Aurelia I hope you have understood this?" Lorenzo said, I just nodded to stunned to speak.

"You guys are gonna be such a cute looking couple," Mom stated. "Ruling the Italian Mafia and of course the American." she and Victoria said. "And hopefully soon there will be a hier." I looked at them with discus. No. Mom and Victoria stifled their laugh seeing my face.

"Well then If there are no more questions." he paused and looked around the room, everybody shook their head. "Then you may go and enjoy this beautiful day" Lorenzo smiled. I got up and left the room and after me Mom, Victoria and Luciano. Dad and Lorenzo stayed behind, probably talking about some other business stuff.

I went up to my room and closed the door behind me. I slid down on the floor and put my face in my hands.

I'm gonna be married soon. Too soon.

12

A urelia Moreno

It was the day we've all been waiting for. The day of the ball. The day me and Luciano would be pronounced as fiancé's. The day everyone would never forget. The day everything would change.

Luciano and I know each other a bit more. And today was the day of the proposal. The ballroom is already decorated and plenty of employees run around the estate, to get done with their work.

I was in my room and some Makeup artist made my makeup "Ok and we are done," she smiled as she put her last brush away. "You look stunning,if I can say that."I look at the makeup which looks so beautiful. I gasp, I've never been that beautiful and that's just for the proposal? What are they gonna do at the wedding?

She did a neutral look, with just some shimmering details. Such as my eyeshadow wich she gave a light pink shade. My lips were colored with a light pink lipgloss and then she did just some highlights with the highlighter at my nose and such.

"Thank you it looks so beautiful" I smiled at her. Just as she was about to reply the door opened and my mom came in with Victoria. As they saw me they both gasped.

"You look so beautiful my dear." Victoria said first. "Yeah you absolutely do." my mom said, smiling as she came right next to me and took a strand of hair in to her hand. She kinda did this since I was little, she would take a hair strand into her hand and curl it around her fingers. It was so soothing, when ever she did this I would feel home.

Mom stood next to me and said "You look just like me ,when I was your age" she smiled, or more like grinned, at me, cringe.

"Mom!" don't get me wrong, I love my mom and she is the most beautiful and gorgeous woman I've ever seen, but who wants to get told that you look like your mom? Well I don't. "Don't say that!" Both Victoria and mother laughed at my expression

"Darling you, of course, are much more beautiful than I'll ever be." she smiled and I could see tears forming in her eyes.

"Mom, don't say that." I said softly hugging her. And just as Victoria wanted to say something the door opened again. It was Sofia, she gushed at me.

"Okay Aurelia, but you look so beautiful, you look just as if you're getting married today. It's only your freaking proposal." she gave me a tight hug. I smile at her. Victoria had told her the news two days ago, and she flipped out. She basically said something with, Why didn't you tell me? And since when? And why didn't I knew about this? And why nobody informed her earlier.

We talked for a while and soon it was time to get dressed. A maid helped me in my dress, which was beautiful as every time ,but this time it showed more than the dress which I wore at the ball, it showed power. It showed how powerful I am, well my family is or more my future family is. Of course I have much power on my own but not as much as my parents combined, not even as my dad alone or my mom. But I knew that this would change as I would get married in some days more like one and a half weeks.

It's a navy blue elegant long dress. The dress sleeves are short, just like a bra strap. It's silky and has a stylish V-neck, just so my boobs wouldn't fall out. It is pretty comfortable for a dress. I wore some heels and some jewelry. My jewelry consists of some golden earrings, with a matching necklace.

After finishing the last touches I went outside. There stood my mom, Victoria and Sofia, which were the only people I saw of this family today, weird. Normally dad would at least check on me when he knew that I was awake. Not even my Cousin was there, nor my aunt or uncle whom I normally would see once in a week, but I haven't seen them since we got here to Italy.

"Okay Aurelia, we have to go, your Father, Lorenzo and Luciano are already there" my mom said. Firstly the party will start at a beach somewhere here in Italy. It was Sofias Idea after she went there for a morning walk. And after we would have been there for some hours and all guests would have gathered, then we will go back here and party here in the ballroom.

Soon we got in the car and went to the beach were everything will start.

"Are you exited?" Victoria asked, as she saw my leg bouncing up and down. No much more anxious I would say. Some really important businesswomen and men will attend this Party and so many eyes would be on me.

"Not really, more anxious." I state and smile at her, she just nods in understanding.

"Aurelia you will drive with Luciano to the party, and we will drive alone. Your father just texted me and said that many guests are already there. I hope that is okay?" Mom smiled at me.

"It's okay mom." I say, smiling at her as she smiles at me.

It is not okay, mom knows how I hate situations like this. Okay the thing with the proposal is new but these balls with the many people aren't. And now with even business partners of my Dad and of course Luciano and Lorenzo. I hate it, what if I tell them something that they shouldn't know. I'm gonna be fucked.

Victoria told me more details about the event, such as what people exactly ,with names, were there, which I didn't know before because I don't know many of these people. It's gonna be much fun. Note the sarcasm there. But to my relief my cousin will be there.

We got to a hold and mom and Victoria got out. I was about to getup too but they stopped me and Luciano got in. Okay if I wouldn't say that he was handsome looking then I would lie. Because he was.

He wore some Armani suit, his brown hair was as fluffy as normally and he was freshly shaved.

Okay I'm admitting it he looked fucking hot. He stared at me and I just smiled at him turning my head away, trying to get away from his stare. But I could still feel his stare which brought butterflies to my stomach.

"We are here, Boss." Our driver said, he got out and opened the door for Luciano. I could hear the music playing at the party and people talking. Just as the driver was about to open my door Luciano opened it and helped me out of the car by giving me his hand, which I grabbed tightly, one because of my shoes or heels how you would call them and two because I was hella nervous and uncomfortable.

I smile at the people who were looking at us, or more me.They looked up and down and then to Lucianos hand which helped me out of the car. Now who is the beautiful one, bitches!

Luciano puts his hand on my back and led me to the main party. On our way I could feel eyes staring at me. I looked up and saw multiple women looking at me with discuss and men checking me out with a grin on there faces. Lucianos put his hand into a fist and I could see his veins forming. His hand never leaving my back.

Luciano De Luca

I saw the car holding and my mom and Carolina, the Mother of Aurelia, getting out of the car. My mother greeted me and I kissed her on the cheek. "Please be good to her and don't leave her side, she is a bit nervous." Mom said, and motioned to the car. She seemed a bit nervous too. I greeted Carolina and then went into the car were Aurelia was waiting.

I got inside and closed the door after that I took a look at the girl besides me. Aurelia.

She had a beautiful dress which suited her just right. Her make up was subtle but also not too subtle at the same time. I stare at her some more, while she smiled at me and turned away, but I couldn't.

Soon we came to a hold "We are here, Boss." my personal driver Roberto said. He went outside and opened my door. The first thing I heard and saw were the many people, who seemed to enjoy them selfs. Some of them turned towards me and their eyes widen, I could hear some murmuring and more and more people looked towards the car. Just as Roberto was about to open Aurelia's door I stopped him. "No I'm gonna do it." I said.

I got to her door and opened it. There she was as beautiful as ever. I looked at the girl which was soon to be my wife.

I give her my hand for her to grab which she does as she climbs out of the car. As she was outside everyones eyes went to her and some of them gasped. I smile to myself. I put my hand on her back and guided her towards the main party.

13

A urelia Moreno

Luciano puts his hand on my back and led me to the main party. On our way I could feel eyes staring at me. I looked up and saw multiple women looking at me with discuss and men checking me out with a grin on there faces. Lucianos put his hand into a fist and I could see his veins forming. His hand never leaving my back.

We went towards my parents, they were standing together talking to someone, but I only saw their backs. I saw my Mom smile seeing me and Luciano walking towards them, Dads eyes were following hers and his eyes light up. He smiles and then says something to the people they were talking with making them turn around.

And that's when I noticed that it was my aunt and my cousin standing there. My Aunt Louise looked at me and her eyes widen, "Oh my God, you look so beautiful mon chéri." - my dear. she smiles and hugs me tightly, so hard that I could not even breath correctly.

Luckily Liam noticed that, "Maman, elle ne peut même pas respirer." -Mom she can't even breathe. He laughed at how his mother engulfed me in a hug. Louise took a step back and admired my outfit.

"Liam, but look how beautiful she is," she looked at Liam, "You look so gorgeous." she states.

Now Liam took a step forward and engulfed me in a hug, "I know Mom" he said as he took a step back and looked at Luciano. I have almost forgotten that he was there. Liam took Luciano in this weird ass bro hug. I don't know I just find it weird. They said their 'Hellos' and then my aunt took me aside with Mom to talk about everything, we haven't seen them in two months. And it looks like many things had happened since then.

After half an hour ,of briefly talking with my aunt and Mom, I couldn't stand there and do nothing so I decided to look for Sofia. We hadn't had the time to talk a lot today, and I missed it. Sadly I didn't found her, only some old men who wanted to talk to me and buy me a drink. I think they didn't knew who I was, I just shrugged and went away looking for someone I knew.

I saw Luciano, talking to some men I didn't know. Of course he knew all of the people who were here, I mean why shouldn't he he probably made business with all of them one time. His eyes flickered to me, he still talked with the men in front of him but I think they have soon also noticed that his attention wasn't on their conversation anymore. They turned around and followed his eyes to me, and some of their corners of their mouths went up slightly, lightly smiling.

I catch their eyes and some of them just nod at me. creepy

Anyways I went around more and soon found Victoria talking with some Women, I joined them in their conversation.

The Time went by quickly and soon we were about to head back to the estate, for the next part of the party. I stood next to Luciano and we went, as one of the first people, to go to the car. We were currently walking next to the water as multiple eyes were on us.

And as we were about to go, Luciano took my arm and turned me around and got on one knee in front of me. He took out a box that had a beautiful diamond ring in it. I gasped at the ring. It was just a proposal ring but it looked so fancy.

"Aurelia, I know that we haven't been together for such a long time. Actually only some months" Oh he's a good liar "But I wanted to ask you the question that I wanted to ask you for some time, Will you Aurelia Moreno make me the happiest man in the world, and become my wife" he asked

I faked my happy teary eyes and nodded while saying "yes, yes I will Mary you" we hugged each other and he put the ring on my finger. Then we kissed, yeah kissed, now you must thing that it was the worst kiss I've ever had, no it wasn't.

It was the best one.

But I still don't like him.

It just didn't feel right.

I heard some people clapping their hands while others took their cameras out and flashed some photos of us kissing. We pulled apart and I faked a lovely smile, while looking at him. Soon we had to go, ho took my hand and we went to the car together. I smiled at the people who were still clapping their hands.

Luciano opened my door and helped me in. After that he went to the other side of the car and got inside himself. Luckily the people couldn't see us inside the car. I let out a breath that I didn't know I was holding. I looked at my hand and thought about what just happened.

Now we are one step forward to our marriage. There is still time for our parents to change their minds.

But I don't think they will.

Our mothers are so happy about this and our fathers are kind of enjoying it too? I don't really know. And don't forget the deal our grandfathers had. I still don't know why my grandpa did this, I was always his favorite. He would have never done this. But I can't ask him, as he died when I was 18.

We reach the estate in just half an hour. I see some guests and our parents smiling at us widely. Liam stood next to Dad and watched the car drive down the gateway till it holds.

The car stops in front of the main entrance. Luciano was the first to get out. He went straight towards my door and helped my out. My heels clicking as we walk towards where all the guest were standing. I politely smile at them although I don't really know most of them.

"Well congratulations on being or becoming a part of our family" Lorenzo was the first to talk to me. "I'm so happy that you are gonna be my daughter" Victoria said, I smiled back. I didn't like this.

"Honey come here" my mom said, giving me a hug. I can see the tears in her eyes. But she tries to hold them back. She tries. And then she starts to cry into my shoulder. "You are such a big girl now. You won't even need me anymore and soon you will have your own loving family." she wishers.

"Mom it's okay, we will still see each other frequently. And besides you still have dad, you won't be alone" I said trying to stop her from crying. She pulled away and laughed lightly "Sweetie you know that I don't like the company of your dad as much as yours." she smiled at me, wiping her tears away.

"Hey, I heard that," my Dad huffed. "It was a joke, Obviously." my mom smacked his shoulder "Or not" she said under her breath, only I heard it. I chuckled at them and looked at Luciano as he was gratulated too.

My dad gave me a big hug with out saying anything. That was just the way he told me that he'll miss me way too many times. He is not the type of person to say lovely shit, like my mom. This is his way of saying sorry or that he's happy for you, it could basically mean everything you just have to connect it with the situation that you are in right now. And I think he wants to tell me he is sorry and happy at the same time for me.

I pulled away and faced the last person. Sofia, who already smiled at me.

"Oh my gosh, we are gonna be sisters" she squealed "I'm so happy that you found your real love even though it's my asshole of brother." Well, who's gonna tell her? I-

"Yes" I said back hugging her tightly, like my life depended on her. I wasn't really the big hugger but if I liked that person then yeah, you can see.

We pull away and my aunt hugs me, just as she saw that nobody was hugging me. Gosh how I've missed her that last two months. "I'm so happy for both of you." she smiles, and sniffles lightly. Yeah she is definitely my Moms sister, both of them are so emotional. She takes a step back and lets Liam engulf me in a hug.

"Dis-moi juste quand ce connard fait quelque chose dont tu ne veux pas et je jure devant Dieu que je lui arracherai la tête. -Just tell me when this fucker does something that you don't want and I swear to god I will rip his fucking head of" I chuckle at his behavior, he was always like a big brother towards me. Liam is two years older and we know each other since my birth. We were always treated like siblings. He took a step back and congratulates Luciano.

After that Luciano took my hand and we both went inside, hand in hand. Other people came towards us and gratulated us. Time flew by quickly and soon, it was fucking 2 am, and everybody was heading home.

I went upstairs into my room, exhaustion taking over me. I could just take my dress and shoes of and then I fell into my bed. After just some minutes dark took over and I fell asleep, dreaming about the events of today.

14

L uciano De Luca

It's two day after the proposal.Nine more days till the day were everything changes. The day nobody will forget. The day me and Aurelia will be pronounced husband and wife. The day we will legally marry, but not wanting. Our Marriage.

I was with my best mate ,Antonio, on my way to get the rings. I actually haven't bought a ring yet, which Mom didn't approve of. She said that it'll be way more stressful to search for one in the store with all the other options. But I don't really care I will take the first one, which I think looks appropriate, and walk back out. Well that was my plan.

Getting inside the store with all my bodyguards, which cleared the store before me entering, I saw a lot of rings. Way more than expected. Well that's gonna be a rough time. "Hello, could I help you?" A women, in her late 50s asked.

"Yeah, actually I am searching for an appropriate ring for a wedding?" I said, well more asked. I didN't really know what was and what wasn't appropriate.

"Oh yes we have a lot for those occasions, follow me." She walked towards a part of the store, where many rings where laid on display, "I actually have a lot more in the back. I will quickly bring them here if you won't mind." She said and walked into the back. Soon she was back and brought some more expansive looking ones.

I just wondered around the store for some minutes, looking at all the rings on display. I found some rings pretty fast but they weren't the perfect one. One was silver with a white diamond on it the other one was prepped with diamond all around and the last one was golden with a majesty Cristal.

They were beautiful no doubt but they weren't the perfect. So I look around a bit more untill.

"Hey look at this one isn't it beautiful, it's perfect for her" Antonio said pointing at a golden ring with a diamond, that wasn't too big but too small either, next to it was the matching one without the diamond. This ring was perfect for her, it wasn't an eye catcher but it wasn't indiscernible either.

"I'm sorry, but this ring is already sold, but we have different ones which are somewhat the same. If you would take a look at these." the lady ,who helped me pick out a ring, smiled. She got out a box with two rings. They didn't look somewhat the same, these rings were the opposite, if that's even possible.

"What do these costs?" I pointed at the ones which Antonio showed me.

"I'm sorry, but these are already sold. But I can show you-" I cut her off "I'm not asking for different once, I want to have these. So please tell me how much the person pays for them and I'm gonna give the double"

"But-" I cut her off again "No buts, I insist to buy these not anything else."

Aurelia Moreno

I was currently sitting on my bed with Sofia. We were looking for a wedding dress for me and at the same time a dress for her online. I don't want to buy one online, I just want to get some inspiration. Mom said that we will buy one in a store ,here in Italy, in some days.

"Oh my gosh, look at this one!" Sofia pointed at a white lace dress, it was strapless with a cute V-neck, the dress itself was floor length with an adorable looking vail. I loved it.

"I love it" I breathed out. I thinks it's going to be a cute wedding dress.

"I know right, it looks breathtaking. If you won't have a dress like this for your wedding than I'm not going" she smiled, she put the dress into the shopping cart and got back to looking for her dress.

"What are you doing?" I asked, looking at her.

"Buying it." she shrugged, scrolling through the other hundreds of dresses.

"But you know that mom and Victoria said that we are not going to buy a dress online." I pointed out.

"But It looked so beautiful," she said.

"I know, but that's not..." I groaned, she hushed me.

"And what are they going to do, I think it will look beautiful on you." she said and after some more scrolling and putting stuff into the card she bought it.

"Let me at least pay," I said, but she didn't stop in her tracks.

"No you don't have to." she shrugged, "But you are paying for my wedding dress." I pointed out.

"It's not even my money. It's Lucianos he won't mind and if he will then all this would change as soon as he sees you in this dress." she smiled and clicked the buying button.

Hi! I'm sorry this is a really really short chapter, I didn't know what to write here anymore.

15

"It's not even my money. It's Lucianos he won't mind and if he will then all this would change as soon as he sees you in this dress." she smiled and clicked the buying button.

Aurelia Moreno

It's 4 days after I've bought my dress online, meaning that it's only 5 more days till the wedding. Okay more like Luciano bought the dress online. In the end he payed for it, but does he know that Sofia bought it? Probably not.

Currently I was sitting on an arm chair, in a little boutique. Mom and Victoria found it after they have been shopping for their proposal wear. I'm going to get my dress customized, because it was a little to big around my chest and my stomach, originally I thought it would be too tight but oh well. Anyways my Mom and Victoria were with me and Sofia of course too, but she was the only one who saw me already in the dress. So Mom and Victoria were really excited.

"Ms. Moreno, you may come in now" the owner said, she was an old lady, I would say in her 60s. She was very kind and gave me very good advice in buying a dress online. She even showed me some of the dresses she has in her shop, which were all beautiful. I even tried some on but couldn't find one that was perfect fitting.

"Thank you" I smiled at her. We got in and she helped me in the dress. Then she took pins and pinned off the fabric that was too much. She helped me out the dress and said that I should take a seat because it would take a while. So I got out and took a seat next to Sofia ,who sat on her phone playing some dumb games.

"Why aren't you wearing the dress, darling?" Victoria asked a bit sadly. "It will take a while till she is finished" I smiled at her. I was really nervous seeing the dress finally perfectly fitting. I hope it would look as beautiful as on the woman wearing it in the photo.

After some moments of waiting she finally finished. She asked me to come inside the changing room and again and helped me in the dress.

"Here you go, there is a mirror." she pointed at a floor length mirror inside the changing room. I thanked her and went in front of it to look at myself. I looked stunning. The dress fits perfectly, it was not too tight neither too loose. The old lady even stitched a little bit at hips so it wouldn't look clumsy.

"Oh my... Thank you so much" I smiled at her, while she smiled at me "Thats nothing, it was really just a little bit of stitching down." she smiled at me and pointed where she made the dress smaller.

I got out of the changing room to show them the finished dress. As soon as I came into their view they gasped. My mom even started to tear up. Sofia grinned from ear to ear, as she saw the dress and mouthed 'I said so', I just chuckle at her and turn to Mom and Victoria.

"You look so stunning, sweetie" Oh no not again. I went to her and engulfed her in a hug. "No don't hug me I'm gonna ruin the dress" she said pointing at her mascara which was smeared at her eyes. "I don't care" I said and hugged her even tighter. Mom tried not to ruin the dress and stepped back.

"Darling you look gorgeous" Victoria stated "Now we just have to pray that everything is good with Lucianos fitting and then we are ready for the wedding" she smiled. Oh Luciano I almost forgot him.

"That was the final thing on the list, now there is just relaxing for you guys" Mom smiled at me.

Sofia took some pictures with me and showed me a potential dress for the wedding. I loved it, it was just what Sofia would wear. It was a yellow beautiful satin dress, I know what you guys will say 'Why satin again?' It just looks so sexy when you wear it that you can't resist to buy one or more.

She bought it and told me that it would be here in two days just enough time before the wedding. I smiled at her and went into the changing room, to change out of the dress into my normal street wear.

"Aurelia," Victoria said, I turned around and look at her. She was smiling at me and held something in her hands. "Here," she said and gave me a beautiful necklace, "This necklace has always been in the family. The Mothers give them to their daughters in Law and today it was my turn. Maybe you can give it your future daughter in law or if not your own daughter." she smiled at me.

I just looked at her too stunned to speak. "The necklace is .... so beautiful." I said, and looked at it a bit closer. It looked very expansive. How could they even wore it, and to what occasion?

"Yes it is," Victoria smiled at me. "I thought that you could wear it at the wedding, as lucky charm." I nod at her and hug her. She hugged me back and I whisper "Thank you," to her.

It is going to be my porte-bonheur -lucky charm.

Luciano De Luca

I was in some little shop were my dad gets his suits and stuff all the time. But right now it wasn't because of him why we were there. It was because of me. My Mother insisted that I should go here for my wedding suit. Preferably a black one.

"Okay Mr. De Luca, we've found some suitable ones for your son" The owner of the shop said, nodding to some suits on hangers. "We've got an all black with a black dress shirt underneath or a white one, which way you prefer. We've also got a blue one just like Mrs. De Luca wanted and a cream one" he pointed at every suit and showed the matching tie or bow tie. I preferred the black one of course with the white dress shirt but Dad said that I should try the rest on too.

"Okay so do you may want to try this one first" Dad said pointing at the blue one, which Mom selected. I nodded and took it into the changing room.

Some minutes later and I was outside of the changing room showing my dad the suit. He shook his head in unapproval. He told me that it didn't look suitable and pointed at the black one that I wanted and said that I should try this one. So I got back inside the changing room and changed to the black one with the white dress shirt. I got out and he look at the employee next to him and then said something. Some seconds later and he came back with a black tie giving it my father.

"Here put this on" he said giving me the tie. I put it one and looked at my dad as he smiled. "Yes that's it" He smiled at me "We will buy this one" he pointed at the suit and the owner nodded. I got changed and handed the suit the employee who was waiting. "-Yes and I want the exact same ones just with a black one and the ties too, thank you" my father was currently talking to the owner at the cash register.

"For who?" I asked him, he turned around "For your best mates of course" he smiled. I paid everything and then we went back into the car. Dad, of course, was really slow because he was on his phone probably texting Mom to tell her that everything went okay and that we have the suits.

I sigh, he can't even walk and text at the same time. Every time when he types he has to stop walking, I saw his bodyguards abruptly stopping every time he stops. I chuckle, they must be as annoyed as I am about this. I think that's the next thing I have to teach him, texting while walking. He taught me so many things, such as shooting, fighting with you bare fist or how to be as quiet as you can be while walking, and now I'm teaching him about the modern stuff.

Thank y'all for the many reads, also please follow my tiktok were I post a video everyday!

I hope that you had a great day or week,tootles!

16

Aurelia Moreno

I'm getting Married.

I'm currently sitting in the dining hall just eating something for breakfast. Mom said that I should eat something before the wedding because it could get really stressful. So I did as she said and ate something ,while the whole mansion is in stress I'm eating relaxed my breakfast. All the employees are running through the halls to get everything ready for the wedding party tonight, which is gonna be here. They started to decorate days ago and are still not finished.

"Ms. Moreno you have to get ready, it's 10 am." one of the maids came to me. "yeah I'm coming" I smiled at her and followed her to an extra room were I would get ready for today. Inside were already my hair stylist and makeup artists. First they did my make up. They put on some concealer which was my perfect skin tone, I'm wondering how long it took them to find the perfect one because you can't buy it anywhere.

Anyways my lips were in a shade of red and my eyelids were a nude color with a bit glitter, I'm not a fan of the glitter it goes into my eyes all the time and it's fucking annoying. But surely after half an hour we are finished and my hair stylist can do my hair. She just lightly curled it and put it in a low loose bun. But it's pretty.

And soon it was time to put the dress on, three people had to help me considering that the old lady in the boutique could do it on her own. What a cool lady.

After I was finished it knocked on the door "Come in" I called while the makeup artist did my eyelashes. My Mom and Dad came in. Mom looked as beautiful as ever and Dad, well Dad looked like this everyday. Mom smiled at me "Hey. honey I, or we, just wanted to check on you" she stood next to me and looked at me through the mirror "Tu es magnifique." -You look stunning. she whispered to me smiling "Et toi aussi." -And you do too. I whispered back.

"Guys that's unfair" my Dad said coming next to mom, we both chuckled.

"Okay Ms. Moreno, I'm done here. Have fun" The Makeup artist said smiling getting ready to leave "Thank you so much" I said "No problem" she smiled closing the door after her.

Dad looked at his watch "Well it's time, Carolina you'll have to get going" Dad said looking at Mom, who looked back at him and then at me with a sad look on her face.

"Okay bye honey, I'll see you in the church. I'm sitting in first row" she said as she hug me "Okay bye Mom" I called after her as she exited the room. I looked at myself in the mirror, I looked beautiful.

"Aurelia darling, where is your bouquet?" Dad asked looking around the room. "It should be here" I said standing up and looking around. "Where have you seen it last ?" Dad asked "Right here" I pointed at the sofa were Sofia put it just some hours ago.

"Look here it is" I said picking it up, it had white and red roses and the other green stuff which a wedding bouquet normally has. Dad picked up my veil "Here I'll put this on and then we have to go" he helped me on putting the veil on my head. "Oh I almost forgot" I got the necklace Victoria gave me, while we bought the wedding dress, and put it on. I can't forget it, I hope that it brings luck.

"Okay I'm ready" I smiled, Dad puts his elbow out for me to take which I did and we walked to the car which would bring me to the church. The drive was short and soon we got to the church. Dad stepped out first and then opened my door, for me to step out. I smile at him and put my arm through his. Sofia and my other brides mates, with some children, were already waiting for me.

"Ma petite fille se marie, je ne peux même pas imaginer ça" -My little girl is getting married, I can't even imagine that. He said, he never talked French. My Mom only taught him a little bit while they were on their honeymoon. He doesn't understand it really well, so me and Mom take this to our advantage. Sometimes, when I was little, we would casually speak French with each other so Dad would be really angry that he couldn't understand what we where saying. We always laughed about him, but I think he learned a bit more. Maybe he had time ,while we where here, to learn some French.

We got in front of the door and I could hear the music playing inside the church. Some minutes later the door opened and me and my dad walked inside. His elbow for me to take. In front of me where little kids who threw flowers and behind me were kids holding my veil up so it wouldn't get dirty. I looked ahead were Luciano stood his hands behind his back and his eyes fixed on me. He wore a black suit with a white dress shirt and a black tie.

Next to him were his groom mates who basically wore the same just black dress shirts.

I could also see Sofia and my other bride mates walking to the other side of where the boys stood and soon I was there too. My Dad gave Luciano my hand and gave me a kiss on my cheek, told Luciano something and then went to his seat. Luciano took my hands and we stood in front of the priest.

He talked a bit, more like too much and then we got to the part were we had to talk.

"Luciano De Luca please repeat after me" he said "I, Luciano De Luca, take you, Aurelia Moreno, for my lawful wife, to have and to hold from this day forward, for better, for worse, for richer, for poorer, in sickness and in health, until death do us part. I will love and honor you all the days of my life."

Luciano repeated everything and Now it was my turn.

"Aurelia Moreno please repeat after me" he said "I, Aurelia Moreno , take you, Luciano De Luca, for my lawful husband, to have and to hold from this day forward, for better, for worse, for richer, for poorer, in sickness and in health, until death do us part. I will love and honor you all the days of my life."

Some little kid brought our rings and he put mine on while I put his on.

"I now pronounce you as husband and wife" the priest said "You now may kiss the bride" the priest said. Luciano looked in my eyes took the veil of my face and kissed me. His one hand was on my cheek while his other was on my hip holding me steady. After some seconds I kissed back, our lips moving in sync. I hear the cheering in the background and the we both pulled away turning to the audience, smiling at them.

I was married

I'm Aurelia De Luca

Hi guys, I hope that y'all liked the chapter. Sorry that I wasn't that active in posting the last days, I was just busy a lot. Bad news I'm not even finished writing this book and there will be at least one more... 03/01/2022

17

A urelia De Luca

I was married

I'm Aurelia De Luca

I'm the Donna of one of the most successful Mafias on the word.

The Italian Mafia.

After the kiss everything went fast. We went outside of the church and were immediately gratulated by some of the people who have been waiting outside of the church for us. Luciano and I thanked them and smiled at everyone who was there. He placed his hand on my lower back and whispered, "Okay beautiful, let's get this done with. Shall we?"

Did he just call me Beautiful? I looked at him stunned, he just chuckled and led me towards the car with one hand on my waist.

We got into a car which would drive us in a slow speed to the mansion for the wedding Party. Where we would meet all the people attending the ceremony and of course our family, all of them would gratulate us and wish us a happy life together. For ever.

The car took a hold and soon Luciano got out of the car and opened my door. He helped me out by giving me his hand for me not to fall. I gladly took it and hopped out of the car. The chauffeur drove off and we went inside the big ballroom of the estate. It was lovely decorated with white roses and other white stuff. On the tables were white Tableclots and some bouquets of flowers, Roses, Peonies, lilacs and Hydrangeas. They were all matching with the theme of the party.

Luciano led me to the "head" table, where we would sit with our parents directly next to us. We hadn't even time to sit down when the first people came and gratulated us. Mom was one of the first. She came walking towards us a smile on her face with a tissue in her hand and her arm linked with my dads.

"Félicitations chérie, je suis si fière de toi. Tu étais si belle debout là." -Congratulations Honey, I'm so proud of you. You were so beautiful standing there. she rumbled as she hugged me. "Merci maman" I said awkwardly hugging her back. "Aurelia I'm so proud of you and I wish both of you happiness and health for your life." my Dad smiled at me "and I would hug you if your Mother wouldn't already" He pointed at mom who was still hugging me.

Dad firstly hugged Luciano, more like a pat on the back if you would ask me, and then hugged me after Mom let go and hugged Luciano. Victoria soon came with Lorenzos arm linked with hers and Sofia behind them, smiling at me. "I'm so happy for both of you" Victoria smiled hugging me and then Luciano, "I'm so proud of you guys" Lorenzo said as he hugged Luciano "And you Aurelia looked so beautiful" he said as he hugged me.

"Luciano," Victoria said sternly, "Sto solo dicendo che se ferisci la sua bella anima-" I didn't understand what she was talking about, but she couldn't even finish as Luciano cut her off, "Mamma non lo farò, lo prometto" Ugh why can't I just speak more then two languages. I want to understand what they are talking about. He whispered something into her ear and she seemed pleased and hugged me one last time, glaring at Luciano.

After they were gone Sofia went towards me and engulfed me in a big hug. "Welcome to your new family" she said "We're like sisters now, I can't wait till you're moving in with us. We could have-" she got cut of by Luciano "We're moving to America Sofia, it's much more safer there for us than here." he said glancing at her. Why couldn't we take her with us, if it's so much safer there?

"And what is that supposed to mean. You guys could also take me with you to New York." Sofia said and went off to her parents. Luciano just looked after his sisters and then went back to greeting people and shaking hands. I just stood there bored out of my mind.

After greeting all the people it was time for the cake. Luciano took a glass and a knife and knocked it lightly against each other so that it was quiet. "Hello guys, I and my wife are both happy to have you here. We want to thank our families who enables all this for us and of course our friends." After a long boring speech, we finally cut the cake. Photos were taken and Videos too as we struggled to feed each other with a fork.

The cake actually was good. After the cake we went dancing. The first dance was just the bride and the groom. Luciano took my hand in his and his other hand was steady on my waist while we swayed through the room, eventually more and more people joined so we wouldn't be the only one dancing.

The second one was daughter and Father dance. Me and my Dad danced together while Luciano watched us more like stalked us. After dancing was dinner. I sat next to my Mom who sat on my right side and of course Luciano who sat on my left side.

We got home at like 1am or something like that. Home for now is a mansion not so far away from our families, in Italy. Luciano took my hand and showed me around for a bit. It was actually cute. I didn't like the decoration to much but we would not stay here this long anyway. This would be our house in Italy. Till the new mansion, how Luciano liked to call it, was built. We would spent here our time when we would visit family here. It wasn't too big or too small either. Just the perfect size for two to three people. Thats what Luciano told me.

He showed me our bedroom, yeah you've heard that right our room apparently this estate only has one bedroom which I'm not buying from him.

After the rest of the tour and introducing me to the maids, cook and some of my bodyguards, we went to our room. I was the first to change, I got into the bathroom and showered first then changed to some pj's and did my skin care routine. After I was finished I went back into the main bedroom and let Luciano take his turn in the bathroom.

I laid on the bed and tried to close my eyes, because I'm fucking tired. After some time I finally fell asleep and heard the bathroom door unlocking.

Luciano De Luca

The Woman standing next to me ,in the church, right now is now my legally married wife, Aurelia De Luca. Donna of the Italian, American Mafia.

We just went towards the table where we will be sitting and guests came towards us gratulating us. I ignored the most of them and just shacked some hands and smiling nodding my head. Aurelias parents came towards us. Coraline firstly went towards her daughter and told her something I French, to which Aurelia responded with "Merci maman" which I could understand because it's easy.

Though I kind of wish that I could understand and maybe speak a bit French. Leonardo gave me a hug and ,after Coraline stepped back from Aurelia, went to her and gratulated her. Coraline gave me a hug and then my parents with my annoying sister came towards us.

Moms arm was linked with Dads and Sofia behind them, all of them smiling at her. "I'm so happy for both of you" Mom smiled hugging Aurelia and then me, "I'm so proud of you guys" Dad said as he hugged me "And you Aurelia looked so beautiful" he said as he hugged Aurelia.

"Luciano," Mom said sternly, oh no she will give me her talk again. She already gave it to me twice. "Sto solo dicendo che se ferisci la sua bella anima-" -I'm just saying if you hurt her beautiful soul- she couldn't even finish as I cut her off, "Mamma non lo farò, lo prometto." -Mom I'm not gonna do it, I promise.

"I will make sure that she is safe. I won't let anybody hurt her." I whispered into her ear and she seemed pleased and hugged Aurelia one last time, glaring at me.

Hi guys it's been a while, I hope that you liked this chapter. Anyways I made some more Book covers so be sure to check them out and vote for the a new one, because I'm honest I'm kind of tired of the current one, so im going to change it.

Anyway until next time,

toodles <3

18

A urelia De Luca

I woke up to the birds chirping outside and the sun creeping in the room through the curtains. It was lovely weather outside perfect for a day at the beach. But unfortunately I can't go there me and Luciano will go back to America today, with Mom and Dad of course.

I rolled over to look at a person next to me sleeping. I was frightened but then remembered that I'm married and that we unfortunately had to share a bedroom. I looked at him as he peacefully slept, lightly snoring as his hair was in his face. I couldn't comprehend what I was doing when I lightly pushed the hair out of his face. He stirred a bit in his sleep, so I panicked and pretended to be asleep.

"I know that you aren't asleep Aurelia" he chuckled lightly. I opened my eyes just to find his eyes staring at me. I smiled sheepish and got out of the bed.

"Haven't said that I was" I said as I walked into the bathroom. I closed the door behind me so I could take a shower and go to the toilet. Firstly I used the toilet afterwards I brushed my cloths off and went inside the shower.

As I washed my hair I thought about how peaceful and beautiful he- No now that's to much.

After some minutes of just standing there and letting the water patter on my body, I decided to get out and brush my teeth and make my hair. As I was finished and wanted to change myself but I found out that I didn't even took any clothes with me. I'm so fucking dumb. I cursed at myself as I tightened the towel around me ready to go out of the bathroom.

I opened the door slowly just to find Luciano laying in bed on his phone, perfect maybe he will be a little distracted so I could easily get back in the bathroom without him seeing me. But of course it didn't work like planned.

Firstly everything was good I got into our closet and searched for something to wear. But as I was about to go back I saw him standing in the doorway watching me. "What are you doing?" I asked, trying to push past him. "More like what are you doing?" he asked as he didn't let me go through the door. "Just searching for something to wear" I shrugged, finally getting past him and rushing into the bathroom as fast as I could, so I wouldn't have to talk one more word with him.

After locking the door and checking if it was really locked, I changed and then did my quick makeup. And then I had to go out to eat breakfast and face him. Well, staying in here and not eating doesn't sound as bad as it is.

I unfortunately am so hungry that I had to go, so I opened the door and saw nothing. Nobody was there. I'm so lucky. So I went to the kitchen although I almost forgot the way I made it. As I got there I saw the cook cooking some delicious breakfast. "Good Morning Mrs De Luca." She smiled at me. "Morning" I smiled back. "You can go to the dining room, Mr De Luca is waiting there for you for breakfast." Oh no.

"Thank you," I said as I made my way to the dining room. Inside I saw Luciano in a white dress shirt, which sleeves were buttoned up so his muscles would show. He was enjoying a coffee while reading something on his phone. I sat across from him and firstly looked at the different food they have. I took a variety of things and then began to eat while Luciano just looked at me.

Luciano De Luca

I couldn't get her off my mind since the moment when she came out of the bathroom in just a towel. She looked so beautiful. I wanted to kiss her and- No where are your thoughts going?

This is just an arranged marriage, nothing big is going to happen between us.

I sat in the dining room just waiting for her to start eating breakfast. I had peacefully read a document my father send me on my phone when I hear her coming in. She sat across from me and took a variety of food while I just stared at her, the pictures of this morning not going out of my head. She glanced at me while eating, her beautiful eyes looking at mine and then she looked at me weirdly. That's when I realized that I was staring, I cleared my throat and began to eat.

"I have a meeting in a few" I said erupting the uncomfortable silents "You can maybe do something with Sofia, shopping or doing stuff what girls do" I shrugged. "And in the evening we will go to America."

She glared at me "No" No? "I'm gonna go with you" she shrugged now it was my time to glare.

"No you can't go with me, it's something about the mafia." I'm doing this for her safety, and if she would come with me then I'm not sure if I can keep her as safe as she would be here.

"And? Am I not gonna be the new mafia donna?" Well she certainly is...

"There will be many man out of other mafias who are much more evil than you think" Why can't she just stay at home and do a little movie day or something with my sister? Then this would be so much easier, she would be safe and I could do my job.

"But not as powerful as you are" she shrugged, good point. But still she could get hurt. "I'm not going to stay at home" she said.

"And I'm not gonna take you with me" I shrugged getting up, I need to get ready. "I think this conversation is not going to end, anyways I got to go." I said as I went upstairs to get ready, she just sat there and stared at me.

I changed into a black suite and went back downstairs as I heard the TV. I smiled to myself and went to the door. "Sir your car is ready" my chauffeur said ready to drive. "Thanks but I'm gonna drive today, take a day off" I smiled as I took the car keys. I opened the door just to find my black Porsche standing there ready to drive, already opened.

I hoped in and started the engine. It's gonna be a long fucking day.

Thank you guys for 230 viewssee ya,tootles :)

19

A urelia De Luca

Did you think that I would just do as I'm told?

If yes then you are totally wrong.

I got up from the table and firstly looked at my outfit. I wore just some black mom jeans with a black top. Nothing too fancy but I hope that it would be enough. Then I went into the living room to turn the TV on and select some random channel. I closed the door a little so he wouldn't see if I sat there for not. After I was finished I went to get into Lucianos car but I was stopped at the door.

"Mrs De Luca were will you be going?" Lucianos chauffeur, who stood next to the door ready to drive with the car keys in his hands, asked.

"Oh I'm just gonna check if Lucianos car is ready, can I not do it?" I asked tilting my head to the side. If this guy is not letting me go outside to this damn car, then this whole plan would not work.

"Of you can Mrs" he smiled at me politely, and opened the door.

I go outside and find his black Porsche standing there, luckily it was open so I could just hop in. I got into the back seat and hid just so he wouldn't see me. Soon I heard the door open and him getting in, he started the engine and drove off to somewhere.

I could hear cars driving besides us, he's probably driving on the highway or something.

Some days ago I wouldn't have thought that right after my wedding I would be doing something like this. But hey it's really cool and fucking exciting too.

After roughly half an hour he finally stops and gets out, after some seconds I heard the trunk open and something pulled out. I waited some minutes after the trunk was shut, then I got up and firstly looked out of the window. I don't remember this place, it looked like I was in a garage in a skyscraper somewhere in Rome. I got out of the car and dusted my pants.

I looked around some more till I found a door, which looked like it would lead to an office. I quickly made my way to it and looked at the little sign on the door which read office. Well how easy this was. I opened it and went inside, where was a big staircase. I followed it upstairs and took the first door that I saw, which lead to a long hallway.

I walked till I heard talking coming from a big door. I silently snook up to it and listened to what they were talking about. The first voice I recognized was his. "Antonio get these shipments ready for tomorrow we don't have time anymore" he cursed.

"Yes Boss" some boy said, strangely his voice was louder than Lucianos which all made sense when the door opened. And I stumbled into the room.

"What the-" the guy in front of me said and took my arm harshly. "Who are you and for who are you spying?" his voice a bit harsher and louder than before, this took Lucianos attention. He looked at me and then at this guy who practically screamed at me. Luciano quickly got up and pushed the boy away from me taking me behind him.

"What are you doing Bo-" the guy said a bit surprised.

"Antonio, don't talk like this to my wife!" He basically screamed at him, which took the guy who apparently is called Antonio back by surprise.

"I- I didn't know" He stuttered.

"Of course you didn't. Finish the shipment and get away from my eyes!" Luciano spat, pointing at the door. He watched as Antonio left the office and then looked at me, with anger in his eyes. Oh oh here we go.

"I think I got to go. Was fun here." I said trying to get away from his grip, but he held my waist steady.

"Not so fast." He said motioning for the man to leave the office. In here were other man too?

After some minutes all of them left. Luciano got back to his chair and went back to writing on his computer. I sat down on one of the couches in the room and tried to get myself comfortable, which wasn't the case. After minutes and minutes of turning and being bored I asked "And when do we leave?"

Luciano just stared at me and then went back to his computer. "You wanted to participate me at my meeting. I told you that you should stay at home" he shrugged. "Now my question. How did you even get here?" He looked at me surprised.

"Thats my secret," I shrugged. "Well what are we gonna do?"

"I don't know what you are gonna do. I'm gonna finish my job here." he said as he went back to his laptop. There was a knock on the door, "Come in" Luciano quickly said, and then a man came inside who just put some documents on his desk then lightly bowed his head at him and as he was about to go he did the same to me.

Luciano opened the documents and cursed lightly as he read it. Now I was curious. I stood up and went next to him. He didn't even noticed me, I took in the first page. It didn't look good for him. I wanted to read the other side too but then there was a BANG.

I fell onto his lap as I yelped a little bit. Now that was a surprise. Luciano looked at the door and then at the clock which hangs over the door. He cursed under his breath as he grabbed my waist and got up. He put me back onto his chair and took the gun from his waistband as he quietly walked towards the door. He silently listened to what was going on outside and then looked back at me.

"Aurelia we have to get you out of here. So please stay by my side all the time ok?" he asked, more like pleaded me. What the fuck is going on?

I just nodded my head and got up, standing behind him. He opened the door and looked around then motioned for me to follow him. We went down the hallway, where I saw many people lying dead on the floor.

And just as we were about to get down the staircase someone fired their gun, but it wasn't one of us. Luciano took my body behind his, just in time for it to stroke his shoulder instead of me. He took his gun and shot him directly in between his eyes, so the man dropped dead on the floor.

Luciano cursed under his breath and ushered me down the staircase. We ran towards the car and as we both sat down he quickly started it and drove off, leaving everything behind.

20

L uciano De Luca

"Come in" I said and one of my man came through the door and gave me the documents for the shipments of last week. He bowed his head at me and Aurelia before going outside again. I open them and curse. These aren't looking good. I read trough them and it even got worse. Why out of all the shipments had it to be one of my most important once.

I don't notice Aurelia standing besides me until I heard a Bang, and she fell onto my lap out of surprise. I grab her waist and got up and sat her back down. I got to the door and opened it slightly. I could see some of my men dropping dead on the ground.

I had to get her out of here. And don't get her hurt in anyway.

After some seconds of brainstorming what I'm gonna do, I finally ushered us both out of the office into the hallway. She was close behind me as we carefully ran down the hall to the staircase.

Footsteps echoed behind us, I tug on Aurelia's wrist a bit more to tell her that we have to walk faster.

They are here. It was time that I showed them. Show them that they messed with the wrong person. But I will only do it when Aurelia isn't with me, it's too much danger.

And just as we were about to get down to the garage, I heard someone fire a gun behind us. My first instinct was to throw myself infant of her, what I also did. Luckily the gun just stroke my shoulder so there were not going to be serious injuries.

I curse under my breath and hold my hand above the ,now new, wound to stop the blood from creeping out.

I took my gun out of my waistband and shot the man right between his eyes. I ushered Aurelia down the staircase and in the corner of my eye I could see more men running after us.

We finally made it to the garage and both hoped into the car. I quickly started the engine and we drove off to the castle.

I could see cars following us in the rearview mirror. "Shit" I cursed and drove a little faster. The cars drove a faster too and soon were directly next and behind us. "Aurelia get down" I screamed at her. She got down just in time for the first bulled to come through the glass pane.

I heard something rustle and looked down at Aurelia, who had a gun in her hands. She got up and opened the car window on her side. She quickly removed the safety pin and started to fire at the people next to us. The car drove off and slammed into a tree after she shot the driver directly in the head.

I heard a little 'yes' and then she took down the other cars following us, till she had no more bullets. Unfortunately some cars were still following us.

"Aurelia take my phone and call the first person. I can't right now." I said to her motioning to my phone which was in my pocket. She took it out and called the first person.

"Hello?" a sleepy voice asked. Damn how much does this boy have to sleep, it's only 10pm!

"Antonia we are being followed. Send someone to help us we can't take all of them out!" I said as I saw more cars coming up on the highway.

"Yea, just hold on for 2 minutes." he said and then cut off the call. I drove a little faster, till I saw four cars behind us which looked a bit familiar. They took the other cars out while driving fast behind us. After every car was taken down, we drove to the side and got out of the car. The other cars took a hold too and some of the man came out.

"Hey good to see you bro" Antonio said and gave me a bro hug, which I returned. I looked at Aurelia and then back at Antonio. "Who shot the other ones? Because I know you drove?" he asked sternly.

"It was her" I motioned to Aurelia who stood by the car looking at her feet.

"Wait really didn't know she could be so badass" he whispered. Yes she is pretty badass.

"Take Aurelia back home. I have to do something. We will be leaving to New York by 2 am. Be fucking ready because I'm not waiting." I whispered to him, he nodded.

"Aurelia go home with Antonio, I have to do something." I said to her and motioned to Luis who was standing at the open car door, smiling at her. She nodded and got into the car. I mouthed 'I'll take care' to Antonio before he hopped in after her.

I watch as the car, with her, drives of another two cars following them. Then I got into mine and started the engine, one car following me.

Aurelia De Luca

I got into the car, really tired and slung into the seat. Antonio got in after me and ordered the chauffeur to get back to the castle. He looked at me and smiled.

"Luciano told me that you shot at the other cars, that's pretty badass!" He said a bit exited. "Didn't know you could do that" He then took his phone out and was busy with writing to someone. Who could that be?

Anyways I slung my head into the seat and tried to relax myself. Thinking of the things that happened just minutes ago wasn't the best thing to be honest.

I had taken a gun. And shot people with it.

I shot out of a car, like in a movie. We've been followed and attacked.

I just shot several people. I fucking killed them.

I fucking killed people who might have a family. Kids. I hate fucking kids.

You know even though I'm the daughter of the American Mafia doesn't mean that I've shot people let alone killed them.

I looked out of the window, seeing the trees on the side of the highway flying by as we speed into the night. After some time I couldn't keep my eyes open and I fell asleep.

21

- -

A urelia De Luca

I've been woken up by Antonio, who was shaking me and saying my name over and over again.

"Aurelia wake up, wake up. Wake the fuck up." he groaned, maybe I should make him wait some more time. So I closed my eyes again and pretended to be asleep. "Aurelia wake the fuck up or I'm gonna-" he has been cut off by a strong, deep voice.

"Or you gonna do what?" Luciano asks. What does this fucker do here so early?

"She hasn't been waking up for the last hour. And I've been standing here because I can't get her up" Antonio wined. You calling me fat?

"It's okay go home. I'm gonna do this" Luciano sighed, sending Antonio away. I could hear him getting closer, till he lifts me up bridal style and brings me to what I think is our bedroom. I heard a door open and then close, then he climbs the stairs and after some minutes I could hear another door open.

Then I'm put into a warm, cozy bed. He takes my shoe off and then my jacket. Luckily he didn't change anything else and just puts the blanket above my body. I heard him closing the curtains and then changing out of his outfit. I heard a belt and then I felt the mattress sinking a little bit next to me. He got under the blanket and turned the lights off.

Now it's pitch black and silent. I turn around and open my eyes a little bit and am met with his face. I shriek back and nearly fall of the bed but am caught by two strong arms.

"Not so fast Aurelia" Luciano smiled and brought me back into bed. "I know that you haven't been sleeping all along." he chuckled, busted.

"We will be leaving for America in some hours. Our bags are already packed I hope that you are ready to go back." I frown a bit, was I really ready? I haven't even said good bye to Sofia, Victoria nor Lorenzo. "You could sleep on the plane, but I would also recommend sleeping till we have to go." Luciano said while getting up. He looked down at me, as I was laying on the bed watching his moves.

"Okay, good night." I smile up at him, as he turns the lights off. I could hear Luciano going towards the bathroom as I close my eyes to consume the darkness as soon as I could. I got a bit sleepier as time went on, I could hear Luciano come out of the bathroom. His steps came further to me and then I could feel his presence right next to me but I was too tired to even react.

"Good night Love." He says, while taking a hair string and putting it behind my ear.

Luciano De Luca

"Good night Love." I said, while taking a hair string, which was in her face, and putting it behind her ear. God this woman is gonna be the death of me.

I sighed and left the room, to do some last minutes business in Italy. Before we will go on that plane I want to have everything important here done, so I could concentrate more on business there for a week or so.

I went to my office, which wasn't as big as my normal office but it would do for just today. I sit down in my chair and open one of the many files that I have to go through. Thats gonna take a while.

I was interrupted by a knock on my door that I answered with a "Come in." Antonio opened the door and came inside.

"Luciano, your plane is ready. And it's 2 am. You wanted to leave somewhat now..." he said looking down on his phone, while talking with me. He was texting someone, but who could it be? I glance up at him, and then again down at the files that I still had to go through. I sigh and look at my watch.

"Yes, we will leave now. Make sure that these files are taken care of. And stop texting your lover while you are working. It will distract you." I tease as I stand up, he texts something and then puts his phone away staring at me.

"Haha so funny." He mocks. I laugh at him and make my way towards our bedroom, to wake up Aurelia. "And where are you going?" he asks, like the dumbass he is.

"Waking up Aurelia, what else?" I shrug.

"And you want to tell me that I'm distracted by some love. Bro you can't even hide your feelings." he says pointing at me, I just shrug and walk past him. Maybe I'm not the best to hide my feelings, but I'm not in love with someone called Aurelia De Luca. This whole marriage wasn't for love. It was just to please our parents and grandparents.

I walk towards our bedroom and see one bodyguard in front of the door. I placed one in front of the door for safety reasons, I don't want to walk into the room and see that Aurelia had been killed nor kidnapped. I nod at him and open the door, just to see a sleeping Aurelia. She looks so peaceful while she's sleeping.

I make my way towards her and shake her lightly. Damn Antonio was right when he said that he can#t wake her up, she's a pretty heavy sleeper. I shake her some more, and at some point I even thought that she was dead but I could still hear her light breaths.

I decided to just carry her to the car. And maybe she will wake up while we drive towards the airport.

I lift her up bridal style and walk down the stairs, with the bodyguard ,from the door, following me. I saw Antonio again downstairs in front of the door waiting for me, of course on his phone again.

He doesn't even look up and just says, "See, told ya." I just shake my head at his behavior and walk towards my parked car, Antonio following me. I put Aurelia in the passenger seat and close the door, after I've made sure that she is safely in the car.

Then I turn around to Antonio, who of course still was on his phone. Man he and his phone are besties. "Antonio, you'll be following us in one of the cars." Antonio just nodded, I don't think that he understood what I said. "Antonio what have I told you? Put the damn phone down." I say taking his phone.

"Hey," he snaps, "You can't just take my phone, you little-" he can't even finish, as I asked him a question.

"What have I asked you just some minutes ago?"

"Uhm, maybe that I can go home?" God this kid is killing me.

"No, Antonio I did not say that. This phone will be with me till we are at the airport, or even longer. Say bye." I said holding up his phone and then tucking it into my suit pocket, he looks at me as if he is going to kill me any minute, "And now listen to me. You," I point at him "are going to follow us in one of the cars," I point at the cars, which where parked right next to us. "till we are at the airport, have you understood?" I look at him sternly.

"Yes" he mumbled and went straight to one of the cars, as I got into my car. I started the engine and could hear the cars behind us. I look at the sleeping figure besides me as I drove out of the drive way, onto the street. She looks so beautiful and peaceful, I couldn't resist to take on of her hair strings in my hand and put it behind her ear. It is so relaxing, seeing her sleeping just seeing that she is safe.

After just half an our of driving towards a private airport, we were there. Aurelia was still sleeping so I decided to just carry her into our private plane. I get out of the car, towards her door and pick her up. Out of the corner of my eye, I could see Antonio getting out of a car and carrying some bags into the plane.

I put Aurelia down in one of the comfier seats, so she could sleep a bit more, and made myself comfy in one of the others. Soon a Flight attendant came towards me and asked if I wanted to have a drink. I ask her for some martini, and soon she brought it towards me. I took the glass towards my lips and looked at Aurelia. God she is so gorgeous, how could I be so lucky.

The plane started and in some hours we would be in New York, our new home maybe for ever or maybe only for now. Who knows?

22

Aurelia De Luca

I woke up in a plane? Yes right I woke up in a plane.

Firstly I was shocked, the last thing I remembered was being in our bedroom. But then I looked around and saw Luciano sitting besides me in some chair, with earphones and his laptop, probably doing business again. Although it wouldn't be bad if he would just do something fun. But no he has to be the Business man he is and do business everywhere he can.

"Luciano?" I ask, you could defiantly still hear the sleepiness in my voice. His head turns towards me as he heard his name being called. He smiles as he saw that I was awake and took his earphones out.

"Yes?" he asks, looking back at his laptop just after some seconds.

"When do we land?" I asked. I wanted to get off here as soon as possible and sleep in a normal bed. Although I have slept ok, but my back hurts so much and I'm still tired.

He glances at his watch and then turns back to his laptop, before answering, "In approximately 30 minutes." I sigh, why couldn't I just sleep till we would land. Now I have to kill 30 minutes of time before we would return to our new home.

I look back at Luciano and see him again typing away on his laptop, his earphones on. I look out of the window and could see the sun rising. Deciding to just get ready, I got up and went into the planes bathroom. I just splashed some water onto my face, used deodorant plus my favorite perfume and did my quick skincare routine. To be honest I was just too lazy to do my makeup, so I just put my hair in a new low bun and exited the bathroom, looking somewhat fresher.

I open the door and went back to my seat, looking out the window. I sigh and just waited till a flight attendant came towards us and told us to put our seatbelt on. Some minutes later and we were on the ground. We went towards a car and were driven to our new home, in New York. Luciano was all the time on his phone calling someone and talking on Italian, so I couldn't understand him. You know two can play the game.

I took out my phone too, and wrote with my Mom. They were already home, they didn't leave as late as we did, they left at 8pm Italian time.

"Mr. and Mrs. De Luca," the chauffeur called out, Lucianos head glanced up at him. "We are here." he said, I looked out the window on the beautiful house, more like mansion, that stood in front of me. My mouth opened wide in shock. Why would anybody need this much space?

The car came to hold in front of the massive entrance. I didn't even noticed that Luciano got out, till he opened my door and gave me his hand. "Come on, I will show you around." Luciano states, still on his phone while showing me around.

The mansion was massive. There were, two kitchens, two dining spaces, one formal and one informal, three living rooms, many more lounge ares, around nine bedrooms, with bathrooms plus closets, some more bathrooms around the house and even a cinema room, a gym, a fucking library and a fucking swimming pool. I haven't even seen the outside and was already stunned.

"And this will be our bedroom." Luciano states, as he opened a massive door. I walk in my mouth wide open. The room had a high beautiful ceiling with tall ass windows. From one of the beautiful big window you have the view of the massive backyard. The room had three more doors. I figured that one is for the bathroom, which had a big shower, bathtub, of course a toilet and two sinks. The other one was for the walk-in closet, which was large, in the middle was a little sofa and it even had a Dressing table.

Behind the third door was a blank room. Luciano told me that it could be used as a second walk in closet, a private office or a more separated lounge area. The room was cute, it had the high ceilings too, just as the master bedroom. But it gave more cozy vibes than the big bedroom right next door. It even has its own door to the hallway. I think you could do a lot of things with this.

Anyway, we went downstairs to eat some lunch, and then Luciano had to do some business again, as always. I wandered a bit around the house, just so I could remember where everything was. I was even introduced to the woman, who would look after our house when we wouldn't be here. She kindly told me that I could redecorate the house, if I want to, and that she would be here for any questions.

She was a nice lady, maybe in her late 60s. She even got me some flowers, which were my favorite, and some welcoming gifts. Her name is Mary, I don't know her last name because she said that I could only call her that.

Mary originally came from England, but has lived her for quite some time. She doesn't have family here, all of them are back in England but she visits them once a year, when she doesn't have to work.

I thanked Mary for her company, we have been talking till it was dinner time. She is a beautiful kind lady. I let her go home for the rest of the day, we won't be needing her presence for the day anymore.

I walked towards the kitchen, where I saw the cook cooking some fancy meal. I hope that it isn't something like the seafood soup that I ate in Italy. I sat down opposite to Luciano, who was reading something. He glanced up at me and then back down at the file in his hands.

The cook came into the dining room and brought the plates with him, putting them in front of us. To my surprise it was Cassoulet, a classic French dish, it tastes so good. Immediately I start eating, stuffing the food into my mouth. Luciano looks at me amused as he sees me shuffling the food.

"Looks like it tastes good?" he chuckled, I look up at him and nod. 30 minutes were about to pass and I was done. I looked up and saw that Luciano was also close to finishing. To be honest I was full and couldn't eat anything anymore. I just wanted to go to bed and sleep away.

Luciano noticed my state, "You can go to bed if you want, I finish this alone." he glanced at me and then his plate. I nod and made my way upstairs.

I don't even have time to change into something comfortable. I just plopped down onto the bed and the dark over took me.

Please vote, thank youand you might want to follow my tiktok which is linked in my description:) tootles2nd April 2022

23

A urelia De Luca

I woke up the next day, someones arms around me holding me against them like their life depends on it. I try to wiggle out of their grip but that only made them hold me tighter. I sigh and try to look behind me and was shocked at who I saw.

It was Luciano, holding onto me for dear life and nuzzling his face into my neck inhaling my scent. I look at him with wide eyes and just wanted to get out of this bed, though it was comfortable not gonna lie. And he kind of looked peaceful as his chest moved upwards every breath he took.

I decided to just take a pillow and put it as a replacement of mine.

Though nobody could replace me.

And it actually worked he nuzzled his face more into the pillow and sighed as he found his comfort. As I didn't want to wake him up I got up silently and made my way towards the bathroom. I wanted to get ready and eat breakfast, maybe I could look around the area for a bit.

I got into the bathroom and closed the door behind me. After looking at myself in the mirror I'm getting ready to shower, stripping off my clothes. I groan as I see that I was on my period again, some blood being in my underwear. I silently grab some essentials and noticed that I only had a few left, guess I have to buy some later.

I get into the shower and get ready for the day, I hope it's gonna go a lot better than the last days.

After I finished showering, I went towards my closet. On my way I saw that the bed was empty. Maybe he was already downstairs eating breakfast or something like this. I get ready and get some presentable and comfortable clothes on, you know I don't wanna look to lazy but feel comfortable at the same time.

I went downstairs just to see Luciano already sitting at the table, with a coffee in one hand and in the other his phone. I sit down opposite to him and start eating breakfast.

Luciano finally looks up and then down again on his phone, "I have a meeting in a few, so you will be home alone. Don't do something stupid." He says as he types away on his phone.

"I actually wanted to go shopping today," I sighed and looked at him as he halts.

"No you will not." he states as he looks at me and then back at his phone. Connard - Asshole.

"And why shouldn't I?" I ask putting my knife down. I will go shopping anyways, why shouldn't I?

"Because you will not. End of discussion." He said and got up ready to leave for his important meeting. That little bitch. I will not let someone tell me what to and what not to do. And what am I even supposed to do here?

Luciano walks out quickly and I can hear his car driving down the gateway, away to his business meeting.

I sigh and get up, not wanting to finish my food anymore. I will go anyways, so I grab my purse and some car keys and walk to the door.

But before I could even open it, I was stopped by one of the guards, "Miss you are not aloud to go out today instruction from boss." he states and halts one arm out so that I couldn't open the door.

I sigh and look at him with puppy eyes, "I have forgotten some things in my car, can't I get them myself?"

He looks at me and then at the other guard, who nods "I mean yeah, but-" he can't even finish and I'm out of the door on my way to go shopping.

I get into the car and race down the gateway towards the street. And as I was on the streets I could see a car following me, ugh this bitch couldn't even let me have my fun. I shrug it off and drive towards the next mall that I know of.

I park in one of the parking lots and get out of the car, the other car holding directly next to me. The window goes down and one of my personal bodyguards looked at me, "Miss we have to go home-" he starts but I juts glare at him.

"But now we are here and don't tell me that I was driving all the way here for nothing," I snap at him and he gulps. He mumbles something to the driver, who parked next to my car.

"Okay well I think you can go shopping but not for long, and please don't tell boss he will kill us." he said as he got next to me, I nod at him and we walk into the mall.

"You know I never watched your name," I state and look at him. He looks up from his phone and says "My name is John miss." and then John goes back to his phone.

I shrug and went to the first store to buy myself some new normal streetwear clothes. I didn't have much of those and so we went from store to store.

As we were in the second store John got a call from someone who shouted at him so that John was scared. "Yes boss we are on our way home," oh no "yes nothing happened" shit shit shit "no boss, yes I'm gonna give the phone to her," no no no, I shake my head at him but he makes me take it.

"Yes?" I ask a bit shyly, shit why did I have to do this. Why couldn't I just stay at home and do nothing, he had sounded so angry.

"Aurelia," Luciano states sternly, "What have I told you?"

"To not go shopping, but I have a reasonable reason-" he doesn't even let me finish,

"I don't fucking care what reason you have go fucking home, I'm not gonna repeat myself," he shouts at me and I flinch at the sudden outburst of him. Why did he even have to shout at me?

"Yes," I mumble and hung up on him, giving the phone back to John. Well it was a bit fun.

John puts his phone back into his pocket and we both walk back towards the car and get in, driving home. boring home.

Guys I'm done with this book and am planning the next one right now, though at the same time I will be editing this book as I've seen a lot of grammatical mistakes that have to be fixed. I've planned to start posting the second book in summer but I can't guarantee anything. 7th of april 2022 tootles

----

24

A urelia De Luca

I'm a bit drunk.

Okay maybe I'm lying, in fact I'm super drunk. Like I literally can't see straight anymore.

Why did I do this? Why not?

Anyways I was bored so I called Luciano. Again why? I don't know, maybe because I was drunk and bored.

Luciano currently was in a meeting, he has been there for hours and hadn't said a time when he would be back. So I took my phone out and clicked on his contact. It ringed for a second till a voice answered.

"Hello?" His voice asks, a bit irritated, "Aurelia, what do you want I'm in an important meeting right now." He states. I decided to go on one of the balconies, just looking at the beautiful night sky. I could see all the stars clearly with no clouds nothing, a could breeze. The City in the distance with all it's lights could be seen, but there was no sound coming from it.

"Aurelia? What are you doing?" Luciano sighs as I didn't answer him. I could see him putting his hand onto his head, shaking it slightly.

"I'm on the balcony, have you seen how beautiful the sky is today. It's so peaceful, I love it. You know New York looks so beautiful from up here." I giggle walking further towards the railing, leaning myself on it, so I could enjoy this moment more. The railing screeched a bit as I was leaning onto it and I knew Luciano could hear this.

"What are you doing?" He asks me, a bit stressed as he heard this sound.

I lightly laugh at him, "Relax it was just the railing, screeching a bit." I say as I lean more and more onto it. You know I liked the feeling, the feeling of freedom, ease, comfort and happiness all at ones. This could be because of my period or maybe because, "I might jump..." I mumble to myself, totally forgetting Luciano on the other side

"no no no.." I could hear someone mumble on the other side of the line. I look at my phone realizing that I was still on the call with Luciano, I hung up and put my phone away. I could feel my phone vibrating in my back pocket continuously, but I ignore it and just leaned myself more and more against the railing letting myself feel the freedom.

Luciano De Luca

"I might jump..." I heard her mumble, and I instantly started to panic. I rushed out of the meeting room, all men looking at me as I run towards the hallway not even excising me. I look at my phone and realize that she had hung up on me.

My car was luckily parked just around the corner. On my way I tried to call her multiple times, everything going straight towards voice mail. I started to panic as I saw our gateway and quickly typed in my code, nodding towards the three guards who were guarding the gate.

I hope her bodyguards have a fucking death wish. When I will find them...

I park my car, not even waiting for someone to take the keys and rushed up the stairs to the balcony where I think she is. And there she is, leaning onto the railing nearly concision.

I curse to myself and run towards her. She was slipping and I watched her just in time. I pull her against myself, trying to comfort her.

She was shaking uncontrollably and slightly crying. Aurelia looked up at me and even started crying harder. I shush her asI sooth her hair back, swaying her in my arms. We sit down onto the ground and my arms go even tighter around her, trying to comfort her.

"Shhh it's okay, you don't need to cry." She nuzzled her face into my chest, drying her tears with my dress shirt. I don't even mind as her tears stain my shirt and just nuzzle my face into her neck, breathing her scent.

She looks up at me and starts to cry again, "I'm so-sorry," she cries choking on her tears.

"It's okay love." I say and get up, walking towards our bedroom. I see one of my guards standing in front of the door, looking into the distance. Well I hope he's prepared. I open the door and lay her down onto the bed. "Go to sleep, you're definitely tired after such a long ay." I smile at her and caress her cheek.

She looks up at me and pouts, "Can you at least lay down with me." she asks, making these puppy dog eyes which you can't say no to.

I nod at her and lay down, taking her hips and spooning her. I could hear her breath turning lighter and knew that she has fallen asleep in just some minutes. She looked so peaceful in my arms, her breath light and her muscles relaxed as she was deep in her dream land.

I get up to find the fucker who calls himself a bodyguard. I hope that he has a good excuse for this. They can't just look after one girl or more like a drunk girl, and they are freaking three people. It isn't even that hard.

I get downstairs and find them guarding the door. What the fuck are they guarding this door they should be near her, any moment something could happen. Just like we saw just now. I give them a death glare and start heading towards them.

One noticed me and my facial expression and instantly knows that he did something wrong.

I punch the first in the face, "The fuck am I paying you for?" another punch, "You can't even look after one freaking girl," I punch the other one as the one I have just punched lays on the ground, groaning in pain.

"Why where you guys not there and saved her," I shout at them, now punching the third one as the others lay on the ground holding their noses in pain. "You guys have one freaking job, and you couldn't even fulfill it." I kick at now the three people laying on the floor.

"If you this ever happens again, I swear to god. I'll kill you with my own hands." I start to kick them harder, "You guys can go now, you're not needed here anymore. I'll make sure you guys get a different job maybe even in the cleaning team." I step back, slowly looking at the people in front of me.

I hope that they'll have fun with their new job. It's one of the low payed and disgusting jobs you could do in our mafia.

I look at one of the other guards, who were staring at this whole show, and nod to the figures on the floor. They instantly understand and grab them by their arms, drawing them out of the house into one of the staff houses where some of our men are staying to be near the house all the time.

I called Liam, Aurelias cousin who also is one of my underbosses, and told him to organize new bodyguards for her.

"Dude what was wrong with them, they were one of my most trusted ones." Liam sighed, I could hear him typing something on his laptop.

"They haven't kept her safe like they should." I say bluntly, walking up the stairs.

"Luciano those were like the third new group I got for you this week, and it's only Friday." Liam said, "Ramenez-moi Arthur, Gabriel et Leo aussi vite que vous le pouvez. Et dis-leur de faire leurs valises." I could hear Liam shout at someone. I don't understand French but I think that he found some new bodyguards.

I paused in front of our bedroom door and looked down at myself. My shirt was a bit dirty, some blood of the three staining it.

"Okay so I got you Arthur, Gabriel and Leo. They are somewhat new but their families are trusted by your mafia, they are the sons of some underbosses." He says, "Oh and I could also get you Yazia she is one of my most trusted personal bodyguards," Liam says, he probably just found her in his system.

"Yeah send her over too," I sigh, "And when are they gonna be here?" I ask.

"Tomorrow I'm just gonna inform them today then they can pack and I'll make sure that they get on the plane still today. I nod, thank him and tell him good bye, ending the call.

I walk into our room and get changed before joining Aurelia in bed. I spoon her again as this was our favorite sleeping position for the last few days.

Thank you for 300 reads <3 tootles! 11th april 2022

25

A urelia De Luca

I woke up to a phone ringing. Luciano groaned and turned over, he took his phone and answered the call.

"Yes?" his morning voice is so sexy, oh my god. "Yes, send them here to our estate I have to check them myself and then they can start working," with whom is he talking? "No I will come downstairs right away." he hung up the phone and gets up, I just noticed now that he is only in his boxers. I blush as I was looking him up and down, damn his thing is big-

I was cut off by him clearing his throat and smirking at me, he turns around and puts on some pants and a shirt. His fingers go through his hair and after one last look at me he is out of the door.

I sigh to myself and get up, ready to start my day. I don't shower because I'm too lazy, I just put on some deodorant and perfume then change myself. After just some minutes I'm ready for the day and leave our room.

As I was going down the stairs I see four people standing in front of Luciano that I didn't knew. I couldn't even see there faces as they were facing with their back my way, so I tried perking my head a bit but that didn't help.

Luciano noticed me and chuckled at my attempt, he cleared his throat making the four people turn around looking at me. There were three boys and one girl, they all smiled nicely at me. The girl had a hijab on, she looked super friendly and my hopes of getting a female person in our house makes me smile. I'm so exited, maybe because I haven't spoken to a girl in days. And I need to speak to someone who will not interrupt me or cringe at the stuff I say, I mean I only asked if they can get me some period stuff nothing more.

"Aurelia," Luciano acknowledged me, "These are Yazia," he pointed at the girl, who was smiling at me brightly. " Arthur, Gabriel and Leo" he pointed at the three boys, "They will be your new personal bodyguards." Luciano states and I look at him with my brows furrowed.

"Why do I need new ones and why even four?" I ask, the last ones let me kind of do everything I wanted so it was fun.

"Because the last ones didn't do their job properly," he pointed out. Okay maybe they didn't but it was so much fun.

"And then why four?" I ask, why do I need four when it was perfectly good with three last time.

"Because your cousin had four extremely good bodyguards for your safety and they are the most trusted, and after I saw the last ones I thought that it was better for you to have four." he sighs, "Anyways I have a meeting in a few, but I won't be back till tomorrow." He rubs his head and goes up stairs.

I turn back to them and smile, "so can we go shopping?" I ask with hopeful eyes, maybe Luciano hadn't said something to them about this.

Yazia turned towards me and smiled, "I mean it's up to you Miss,"

"Oh no don't call me Miss call me Aurelia," I smile at them and they nod, "Well then let's go."

We walk together outside, I saw that Luciano haven't already left, well I hope that he won't noticed.

Leo opens one of the cars for us and I get into the back with Yazia, while Gabriel gets into an other car and the other ones get into the front seats. We start driving towards the inner New York City.

I and Yazia talk about random stuff on our way like, about our families, where we are originally from, what our hobbies are, and more.

I found out that Yazia is from France, and the other dudes too, I told her that my mom is French too and that I'm half American half French. She also has two siblings, two sisters to be exact, I told her that I was an only child but wanted to have a sibling for so long.

"Oh non tu ne veux pas avoir de frères et sœurs, comme ma petite sœur qui a cinq ans, c'est pas si mal mais ma grande sœur. Oh mon Dieu, nous ne voulons même pas parler d'elle, je veux dire je l'aime mais, je ne sais pas - Oh no you don't want to have siblings, like my little sister, who is five, isn't that bad but my big sister. Oh my we don't even want to talk about her, I mean I lover her but, I don't know." she shrugged and looked at me.

"Tu as une petite soeur? J'ai toujours voulu en avoir un. - You have a little sister? I always wanted to have one." I gasp at her, she laughed quietly.

"C'est un ange même si elle peut parfois être un petit diable. je l'aime tellement. - She is an angel although she can be a little devil sometimes. I love her so much." she sighs and dreams in her memories.

"When was the last time you saw her?" I ask, switching back to English.

"Uhm, about two months. I don't really know," she shrugs it off, as I look at her with a sad smile.

"Why don't you call her when we get back home?" I smile and her face lights up.

"Mais d'abord, nous allons nous amuser à faire du shopping, vous savez que ces gars-là sont les pires à ça. - But first let's have some fun shopping, you know these guys are the worst at that." she laughs. Man if we won't end up being best friends then I'm gonna kill myself.

I laugh with her and we couldn't stop till the boys from the front gave us an annoyed glare. We shut our mouths and tried to still it but couldn't.

After some more minutes ,of just laughing, we finally arrived at the mall. My stomach hurt from all the laughing and so did Yazias, so we bought some ice. Okay maybe it won't help but now we had an excuse to buy some.

We walked through the mall, the boys behind us like the professionals they are, while Yazia and I got best friends. Yay now I have someone to talk to, who isn't ignoring the shit out of me.

The next store we wanted to go in was this one underwear store. Yazia and I needed some new stuff, I did totally not buy everything I bought with Lucianos money. No I would never.

But I hope he is good with the bill he will get.

Anyways we went into some more stores, but after some time it got dark and boring so we decided to just go home and chill for the rest of the night.

As we were in the car, Arthur got a call, "Yes?" he answered, he nodded at the phone the whole time, "Yes, we are on our way back, everything went okay. Nothing suspicious happened," he said. He nodded and gave me his phone, I sighed and looked at the contact. It's saved as 'boss', here we go again.

"Yes?" I asked.

"Aurelia do me a favor and do not buy so much underwear next time," oh no, I blush a bit. "Firstly don't you have enough good brand clothes, which costed a lot of money, and secondly why did you even buy like this cheap stuff?" I blush once more, why is he even checking his bills, doesn't he have enough money to not care about it?

"I wanted to have some no brand stuff and not walk around with brands all the time," I sigh.

"Aurelia, princess, you are one of the richest women on the world," he said sternly, I can't with him anymore, "And-" I don't let him finish what he wanted to say.

"Bye." I state and don't even let him respond. I just jung up on him and gave the phone back to Arthur, then turn back to Yazia who is looking at me with a smirk.

She can't even hold her laughter, and laughs loud out. I smile at her and then start laughing too.

We nearly have 400 reads, thanks y'all. Please know that you matter and that we all love you.Tootles :) 14th of April 2022

26

A urelia De Luca

It has been days since I saw Luciano, nor did I hear something about him. Nobody wants to tell me, they don't even mention him around me. And when I do then they will awkwardly look at each other and come up with a different thing to talk about. It's so annoying how I'm being ignored.

I sigh as I wake up in a cold bed, with nobody who held me this night again. Maybe it was also cold, because December was starting in just as few days, but we will ignore that for know.

Today I wanted to change something on my daily routine. I wanted to do some sport and eat healthy for once, maybe even go outside if I could. If I was being honest, I tried it yesterday already and was escorted back into the estate within seconds. I couldn't even go into the garden.

I made my way towards the bathroom and showered firstly, trying to get my cold body as warm as possible. To be honest, I was freezing since Luciano wasn't at home at night and didn't held me close while sleeping.

Just as I was about to exit the en-suit, someone knocked on the door several times.

"Aurelia, WAKE UP." Yazia screeched, probably laughing her ass off at something. I smiled and made my way towards the walk-in closet. I quickly put on some clothes and walk towards the door while drying my hair with a towel.

Yazia was knocking on the door all the time, I didn't think that she could be so patient. I literally thought that the door would be down till now.

"AURELIAAAAA!" oh there she was, I opened the door and saw her running towards me, probably to get the door down. Unluckily she couldn't stop, she ran towards me and I took her down with me to the ground.

Ouch, with a loud thud me and Yazia were laying on the ground, groaning in pain. I looked towards her and smirked, "Jokes on you, I was awake for some time already." I laughed at her and got up from the ground. Letting the groaning Yazia laying on the ground alone.

I gave her my hand and helped her up, I'm not such a bad friend at all. Personally I would recommend myself as a friend, you know I'm helpful, funny and loving all the way.

"You bitch." Yazia whispered, holding her head in pain. I held my laugher for myself and help her towards one of the couches in the bedroom. She laid her head down and just looked up at the ceiling.

"What did you want so you would have to take down the door anyways?" I ask, what the hell would be so important?

"I actually wanted to be a good friend, and bodyguard, and take you out of this house for once to go shopping. Since you haven't left the house for days." Yazia mumbled, looking at me then back at the ceiling.

"I actually wanted to go out today too," I state, looking at her. Yazias head goes up slightly while she smiles at me.

"Then what are you waiting for?" She says, grabbing my hand and dragging me out of the bedroom towards the kitchen. "But before we go we will eat breakfast, I'm starving." Yazia states and grabs a bowl for her and for me.

While I waited for her ,to bring the rest of our breakfast towards the dining table, I looked around. As always the backyard looked stunning with all it's flowers and the trees, which were ready for winter. I love winter, I really do but I hate seeing the trees so bare. The birds where chirping, which you could here from here, they are probably flying to the south to enjoy the warm weather there, while we will stay here and wait for them to come back.

Soon Yazia came into the dining room, two bowls in her hands with what I think is yogurt and fruits filled. I actually prefer American or French breakfast, but sometimes I even loved the simplest things to eat, like today.

I smiled at her and took my bowl, while she sat down next to me. We ate in silent for some time, till Yazia spoke up.

"You know I have seen this really cool looking outfit, that I wanted for some time. I would really want to go there first if you don't mind, maybe you will find something too." I smiled at her and nodded my head. To be honest I needed some new clothes too.

We finished eating pretty fast and made our way towards the car. Arthur, Gabriel and Leo were already waiting for us, all of them were on their phones minding their own businesses until Yazia cleared her throat.

All three of them looked at us and immediately put their phones away. "Good morning Miss, where do you may want to go first?" Spoke Leo, while opening the door for me. Haven't I told them to call me Aurelia and not be so formal? I think they will never learn it.

I sigh, "Firstly don't call me Miss, call me Aurelia." I state while climbing into the car,

"But Boss said not to-" I cut him off, glaring at him, "I do not care what your 'Boss' said this is a order," I snap, he just nods while gulping hard. I didn't want to say it like this, but maybe they will remember it now, "Yazia tell them the address." I state, she nods and smiled at me while giving the address to the boys, sitting in the front.

Gabriel gets into an extra car, and soon we drove off towards Downtown.

Hi guysThank you for over 400 reads, thats really insane, I never thought that so many people would read this book. Tootles, 22nd April 2022

27

Aurelia De Luca

It has been three days since I have heard or saw Luciano and the sick feeling in my stomach won't go away. I was currently in the kitchen making my own dinner for tonight, Yazia had spent the whole day with me and I told her to go to her room and take a break which she gladly did.

So now I was alone, cooking my favorite dinner, which was also the easiest dinner which can not go wrong. It was pasta more like pre made one, but I made my own tomato sauce to feel a bit more healthier. And for desert there will be chocolate ice cream, my favorite.

I was humming to my favorite music on the speakers when I heard a car driving down the gravel of the gateway. I didn't expect anyone, so I looked outside and saw Lucianos car parking in front of the doors.

I look at the car, my mouth wide a gab, as he gets out of it. The man in all his glory is standing there, giving his car key to one of the guards outside.

Some of his clothes were bloodied and his hair messy as he walked towards the door.

I got out of my shock stare as I heard the door open, and I ran as fast as I could towards it. And there he was looking around the house in search of something. I don't even wait a second and run into his arms, as he hugs me back.

He lifts me up so my legs are around his waist and looks me in the eyes.

I don't even know what happened but his lips touched mine, kissing me. After some seconds I kissed back, as he held me up by my waist his other hand going to my cheek holding it. He smiled into the kiss just as I did too.

We both pulled away slightly and he puts his forehead against mine, "I missed you," we both say at the same time, making me laugh slightly.

He kiss me again but this time more forceful, making out with me. As we were making out he walked upstairs towards our bedroom and it all happened so fast.

Luciano tossed me onto the bed. We made out while he was opening my shirt, I wasn't wearing a bra for comfort. Because sometimes this shit was uncomfortable as hell, tho I had some which were comfortable, today I didn't wore one of them.

He groaned as he saw my boobs and snuggled his face into them. I moaned as I felt his mouth on my nipple, nipping on it while groaning. My body shakes as he kisses, down from my neck towards my stomach.

Luciano holds in his track and looks up, locking his eyes with mine. "I- We don't have to do this you know, I can wait and maybe you want to do this with someone else, I can understand that totally-" He rambles while getting off of me.

I'm getting frustrated and pull his face towards mine, kissing him forceful-ly. "I want to, now." I whisper, earning a moan from him. He grabs my ass, with his hands, and squeezes it lightly. While I try to take off his dress shirt, which I couldn't get off, after some time I got frustrated.

"Take it off." I urge, while he was kissing my neck, probably letting bruises behind. Luciano chuckles at me and slowly raised onto his knees to take the shirt off. I bite onto my lips, as he unbuttons his shirt.

While he was doing so, I rubbed his dick under his pants. He tilted his head back and groaned. After some time, he finally got his shirt off and started to unbuckle his belt. As he was doing so, I began to take my pants off too, only to be stopped by the man himself.

"I want to do that," He said and took the waistband of my jeans into his hands. Lucianos head dipped down and while taking off my jeans, he kissed along all the way down. He threw my pants somewhere in the room and started to take off his underwear, while looking me in the eyes.

As he finished, my eyes swiftly went down. I gasp as I see his length, my eyes went wide and I looked up at him. He just smirked at me, while going down to take off my underwear, which he did in just some seconds. Of course he had to tease me and kissed my inner thighs making me press them together, sadly he stopped me and forced them back open.

Luciano firstly plunged a finger into me, which made me gasp. He moved it around my slit, up and down, collecting my juice. As he got some, a second joined him, but this time he went in and out of my pussy. A finger went onto my clit and rubbed forcefully, making me moan. My whole body was on fire, I felt like I couldn't really breath.

I moan at the feeling of another finger. I think he noticed that I was close and curled his finger inside me making me gasp, while I came. He didn't take his fingers away and rid out my orgasm with me. After I got down from my high he kissed my lips, my legs where still slightly shaking tho.

He groans and spreads my legs, while taking his dick into his hands. He lined himself up with me and pushed in slightly. He's so deep, my eyes are rolling back into my head and I close them. My breaths get caught, while he keeps going into me.

"Open your eyes baby, you almost took everything, just a bit." He states while taking my waist, stopping me from moving.

"Luciano" I moaned as he kept going, and then out of no where he plunged the rest into me, making me breath faster than normal.

I look up at him and meet his eyes, "Just tell me when I can start okay?" I nod and wait a bid, getting used to his size. After a minute or so, I said that he can start. I put my hands on his back, probably leaving marks, as he goes in and out of me.

Luciano stopped and looked me in the eyes, I kept scratching his back. He groaned and takes my hands into his, and put them over my head.

Then he began moving again, I moaned uncontrollable, while he pounded in snd out of me. I arch my back, while he kissed my shoulder, going harder and faster with each stroke.

I was close and I think he could feel it too, my walls clenched around his length. Luciano groaned and lightly bid into my shoulder muffing those. Soon I came, my body became weak and trembled in his hold. I became tired and let my body lay down.

He finished at the same time with me, and cuddled me. We stayed like this for some time, he was still inside me but I didn't really care, I was comfortable.

I fell asleep soon.

Wait guys, we nearly have 500 reads.Thank you so much <3 tootles, 26th
April 2022

28

A urelia De Luca

I woke up the next day, strong arms around my waist. Luciano was protectively holding me like his life depended on it. He was the big spoon, while I was the little spoon.

I smile to myself, as the events from yesterday made me blush. I turn around, so that we were face to face, and began to play with his hair. I just then noticed that we were both naked, since our little session yesterday.

Lucianos grip tightened, as he snuggled his head into my neck, taking a deep breath. I tried to get up, wanting to put on some clothes before there might be a strange tension. After some minutes, I finally got his arms off of me and got up, just to put on Lucianos dress shirt. Then I went towards the bathroom, which I should have done yesterday directly afterwards.

After I got out of the bathroom, I couldn't find the man himself sleeping nor being in the room. I think that he found it bad yesterday, after all it was my first really time.

I sighed and went towards the closet, maybe he was in there getting ready for the day, but of course he wasn't. Instead I got ready and took out some of my comfortable clothes, as I would definitely stay at home the whole day.

After I got ready, I went back into the still messy room from yesterday. I didn't want to let somebody clean this up, so I did it myself. Picking up our underwear and dirty clothes, I felt my heart ache a bit. Why would I be so stupid and think that he actually wants something from me, he probably just wanted to fuck somebody and didn't want to go to some girl because he had a wife.

I sniffled back my tears and put the clothes into the laundry basket in the bathroom, before returning to the main bedroom, where I started to do the messy bed. After I was finished, I opened the curtains and let in some day light. I didn't feel that hungry today, therefor I decided to not eat breakfast and potentially see him today.

Instead I decided to make myself a beautiful day, and stay in bed while watching some comfort movies of mine from my childhood. I snuggled into the covers and turned the TV on, searched for a good Christmas movie firstly, because the Christmas season is beginning right now and laid back down.

After my third Christmas movie, I finally decided to watch one of my comfort movies, because I really needed it now. I even brought myself some chocolate ice cream, which was one of my comfort foods, and started the movie.

As I sang along the intro lines, someone bursts into the room. And look who it is, indeed it was Luciano, who was looking annoyed.

"Turn this fucking tune down, I hate this movie." he shouted, which made me flinch slightly. I fiddled with the remote and as I couldn't do it he snatched it out of my hand, slightly hurting me but I ignored it. "What are you even eating?" he asked in his annoyed voice, taking a look into my half empty chocolate ice cream box.

"No wonder why you are so grassa, when you eat this stuff all the time. You even know that it'S unhealthy. -fat. " he stated as he snatched the ice cream box from me, the spoon still in my hand. I was looking up at him and could feel tears forming in the back of my eyes.

"I decided that we should stop sharing a room, so I got you a room ready. And I decided that you should go there right now," He stated and grabbed my arm harshly, launching me out of our- his bed. I just wanted to get out of this room as fast as I could and made my way towards the door.

"I think you should take some things with you, as you will not ever step into this room again." he stated making me hold in my steps. I turn around and look at him, as he was looking at me motioning towards the closet with his eyes.

I huff and walk towards the door, just taking as many clothes with me as I could carry and began walking towards the door. I wanted to open the door but was bet by him, he pointed outside the door and looked at me reproachful.

I went out and heard the door being harshly shut behind me. I sighed and looked around, nobody was in the hallway. This fucker I didn't even know where my new room would be. So I just took it into my own hands and began walking in the different direction on the bedroom, more like his bedroom, and took the farthest door.

And indeed it was a bedroom, well it only consisted of a bed, little closet and a tiny en-suit. But I still took it, opening the doors of the closet and just throwing my clothes inside, before plopping down onto the bed.

I couldn't help it anymore and began crying. Letting all my emotions out, yelling into the pillow and whimpering until I fell asleep, with still the present ache in my heart.

I woke up after some hours, and looked around the room, hoping this was all a dream. But it wasn't. New tears already forming in my eyes, but I sniffled them back and looked at the clock in my room, 8pm it read.

It was already dinner time, but I didn't feel hungry and just sat there staring around the room. It didn't have such an amazing view like his bedroom, but the view was pretty after all. I enjoyed it for a bit longer, before sighing and searching after my phone so I could watch some sort of movie, as the room didn't have an TV.

But to my luck I forgot it in his room and I couldn't get it. So I just sat in my bed, looking at the wall, waiting to fall back to sleep.

Guys we are nearing the end of the first ever book in this series, i'm so thankful for all your reads and votes,tootles. 29th April 2022

29

Aurelia De Luca

It had been four days. Four days since I have been kicked out by him. Four days since I have talked to anyone. Four days since I have eaten normally. Four days since I have seen him. Four days were I only slept and cried.

Everyone has been ignoring me, probably by Lucianos order. Tho I could see them from my window, and they could clearly see me, they still chose to ignore me and did their work as normal. Even Yazia, who I thought was my best friend, ignored me the whole time.

I didn't have my phone, so I couldn't text Mom nor Dad and maybe talk to them. No nobody thought about me, they didn't even feel like bringing me food, water or anything essential. But maybe it was my fault, maybe they thought that I would come out of my room and take the stuff I need, so they don't have to.

Luciano De Luca

I had to do it, they have found her and I have to keep her save.

Okay maybe I was a bit too harsh. Cut the crap, I was too harsh. I shouldn't have snapped at her at first time and then call her fat, what the fuck was I thinking.

Throwback

I woke up alone, nobody was besides me but I could swear that I had her in my arms just a moment ago.

I groan and got up, looking around the room. The room was a total mess, clothes were lying everywhere. But no sign of her.

I was surprised by the ringing of my phone, groaning I took it and looked at the caller ID. It was Liam, I was somewhat surprised, why would he be calling this damn early. I picked it up tho and was immediately met by a nervous Liam.

"Okay big boy, you have to listen for once. This is about Aurelia," My blood began to boil, what was so important about Aurelia right now. She was safe, with me right now. And haven't I told him to not call me 'big boy' for uncountable times?

"They have found her," He stated, who had found her? And even if they want to do something to Aurelia, nobody is as dangerous as the Italian mafia, so there should be no problem. Except the Russians, but why would they even search for her- "The Russians where searching for her after finding out this one event with Ivanov." My thoughts where cut short.

These fucking Russians, "And what do you want me to do?" I asked, patiently. Liam knows what to do in these situations, he was hired for that after all. Keeping the Mafia boss's family safe.

"Firstly don't get like all attached to her, they would find out way more faster if you did. The Russians don't know her current location, but what they know is that you are married to her. So they will firstly follow you." Liam states, I could hear the clicking of a keyboard in the background.

I sigh to myself, damn how should I do that. Why was this happening right after we became so close?

"I will See what I can do." I state, "And you will come to Italy as fast as you can, to help me here."

"Already in the plane, on my way there." Why was he always so fast with everything, well it was his cousin after all who is in danger, "I will be there in about two hours," he states.

"I will be sending you a car." I state and end the call. Putting my phone away as I get up and change. Sadly Aurelia didn't went back into our room, so I just went to my office to get started with the new mission.

Not get attached to Aurelia De Luca.

Present

Well I messed up really bad.

I haven't seen her for days, nor has somebody else. She had never ever touched the room that I got her ready. It was not directly next mine, only two doors further down the hall. So I would have had her in my reach, but not get attached to her too.

I'm kinda worried, the fact that nobody had seen her since has me even more concerned. We searched about every room in this house, nobody was there, and I was getting kind of anxious.

My family was going to be here in two days, they wanted to spent some time with us before Christmas. Especially Sofia, she had missed talking to Aurelia, she was the one suggest that they would be visiting us. And of course my parents had to agree, as Sofia will go to college in some days and can't visit us for Christmas.

She will go to England for college, or more university, she wanted to go there her whole life but didn't do it till now.

Anyways, we were all searching for her again.

Aurelia De Luca

I felt weak, although I was lying all day around and didn't do anything. I was lying in my bed as I heard my name being called, again. I heard it some days ago too, but thought that that I misheard it adjust brushed it off. But today I was confident that I heard it. Thought it could be that I was hallucinating.

"Aurelia, where are you?" I heard the voice again, it was in front of the door. I could hear doors opening and closing in the distance. And then finally my door opened and guess what.

Yeah, the man himself opened it. He stoppen in his tracks as he saw me laying on the bed, looking up at him. He starred at me, his mouth opening as if he wanted to say something and then closing again.

"Why are you here?" He asked, walking up to me. I looked at him confused, wasn't he the one who was saying that I should sleep somewhere else.

"And most significant, why weren't you coming out of here?" He took my hand in his and kneeled down next to me, looking me in my eyes as I laid there.

My eyes got heavy out of no where, and I felt more weak than before. My head was spinning.

"Hey, hey," Luciano said, lightly patting my cheek, "stay with me Aurelia. Come on." he says panicking. I could feel that I was lifted up, that was the last thing I can remember.

14th of May 2022

30

Luciano De Luca

Shit, shit, shit. I ran out of the room she has been staying in, her laying unconscious in my arms.

"Somebody help, call a doctor." I shouted, panicking. I ran down the stairs and found her bodyguards standing at the house entrance, ready for any danger. Their eyes became big as they saw her in my arms.

One of them took his phone out fast and called the family doctor.

God, how could this happen?

Soon the doctor arrived, he instructed me to put her down and then sent me right out of the room. He said that everything will be fine, but I'm not taking it. I have seen her with my own eyes and she looks horrible.

Now I'm standing her, or more like pacing, in front of my room, waiting for the doctor to come out and tell me that everything is fine. Or even better, Aurelia herself. Nut I know this won't happen. I can't do this anymore, my hands grip my hair as I bang my head against the wall.

Why am I so fucking dumb? I obviously hurt her feelings with what I said and did. Why didn't I just stop, why was I so fucking stupid and let some boy tell me what to do. Tell me that I had to push her away 'to keep her safe', even though I could do this without pushing her away.

I am a fucking Mafia Boss.

What would people think when they here that I couldn't even keep my wife safe? They would think that I'm weak.

I get ripped out of my thoughts as the door opens, Mr. Greco, our family doctor, came walking towards me with a sorrowful on his face.

Oh no, no, no, no, no.

Please, don't be....

"She's in a critical phase right now, Mr. De Luca. I, as your doctor, can not do anymore that I'm doing right now, my hands are bound. But I would recommend getting her to a hospital, there will be better and specialized care for her." He states, I'm not gonna put her in a hospital. Do I look like I would give her in some random persons hands?

"I-" I wanted to start, but was cut off by the man. "I know how it sounds, I will of course still look after her and such, but she has to have someone looking over her twenty-for seven, and this can only be provided at the hospital." Mr. Greco says.

I sigh and turn around, taking both my hands behind my back, pacing around a little more. What If I won't bring her to a hospital, and she won't get the care she needs, but then also what if I bring her to a hospital and then some of my biggest enemies can get very easy and fast towards her.

I now know why my father always told me to buy my own hospital. It would just be safer for all of us, to be able to go to a hospital and be safe.

I turn back to Mr. Greco and nod, "Uhm yes, what hospital would you recommend?" I asked, hating the idea of bringing her somewhere unsafe. Well I guess that it can't get any worse.

"I would obviously get her to the hospital that I'm working at," He smiled and gave me the address. "I'm just going to make some calls, and get a room ready. Maybe it would be good to pack some personal stuff for her." Mr. Greco said and made his way downstairs.

I sigh and get to work, taking out one of my suitcases and packing it with everything I think she'll need once she wakes up, and probably will be leaving me. It's not much special things, just some clothes, hygiene essentials and maybe even two or three t-shirts of mine, which she can use. Only if she wants to of course.

After some time, I finally get the courage and make my way towards our bed, to look at her. And there she's laying, peacefully sleeping with her eyes closed and mouth lightly open. She looks very pale, and skinny. Just as if she only consist of bones and skin, nothing more. I really broke her.

Mr. Greco, again, cut my thoughts off, as he walked in the room, his phone still at his ear. "Mr. Luciano, there are some rooms free, which would you want?" He asked, looking at me as I'm standing there.

"The best one that you have should do just fine," I want her to feel comfortable, even though she probably won't feel comfortable at all.

"Okay, the room will be done by the time we get there." He smiled and made his way towards us, checking her temperature, "Thats not so good, her temperature is rising, slowly though." I look at him, my eyes probably as big as an apple.

I don't waste time, taking her in my arms and carrying her, bridal style, down the stairs. Mr. Greco behind me with the suitcase I packed her. I put her into my car, while Mr, Greco gets in his and tells me to drive after him.

It didn't even take us half an hour and we were at the hospital, two nurses were already there, helping us with the suitcase and bringing us a wheelchair, although I'm perfectly fine with carrying her wot her room, which I did in the end.

As we got towards the room, or more like a little flat, I laid her down onto her bed and let Mr. Greco and the nurses do their work. I just stand there watching as they check their temperature and give her countless injections. They take their time and only after I know that they all left, I got myself to look around the room.

The room was simple, one room for the patient, with the bed, sofa and so on, one little kitchen with dining table, another bedroom probably for guests and a good size bathroom. I also have to mention the beautiful view we have. The beautiful New York skyline and then the hospital Parc right in the back of the hospital.

Only now do I notice that I should've packed myself a suitcase, so I could stay here with her.

Guys the book has OVER freaking 600 readsI'm literally so excited, you don't even understand. But we also nearly finished this book, next week will be posted the last chapter and then the new book will start, though I haven't really started writing the new one so you have to wait for a bit. Tootles:)

22nd May 2022

31

- -

When I awoke the next day, nothing had changed. Aurelia was still lying next me on the bed, her eyes asleep and a slew of tubes dangling from her arm.

I despise myself for what I've done. It's entirely my fault that she's here right now, and that she might not be able to wake up again. It's entirely my fault. I'm listening to the monitor next to her beep. According to the nurses, this indicates whether or not she is still alive.

The beeping suddenly stops.

"Wait, what?" I begin to feel worried "Please, someone, help me! She isn't- she isn't- " I yell, as I open the door. When a nurse peeked out of the break room and saw my terrified expression, she rushed up to me.

"I- the thing, it- it's not beeping anymore," I try to breath, and she rushes past me. "I'm not- I- don't know what happened." I look at her as she works really fast at trying to get her back. Not much time passes and more nurses rush into the room.

"You must wait outside, Mr. De Luca." As he leads me outside, one nurse informs me politely. I go out numbly, seeing the door shut behind me.

I stand in front of her door, waiting for someone, anyone, to tell me that she is doing well. That she'll be back with me in a few weeks, as if nothing had occurred. It hurts me to realize that I was most likely the cause of this. That I was the one who forced her to starve and maybe die.

I'm ashamed of myself. What do you think her parents think of me? They most likely despise me, as they should. Sofia surely despises me as well, and I am certain she will not let this go till I die.

I hate to admit that, but I feel like crying. For the first time in years, I'm crying. I honestly can't recall the last time I cried. I was maybe ten years old at the time, and I couldn't show any emotion after that. To keep myself, my family, my friends, and, most importantly, my most loved ones, save.

I did everything possible to protect the person I.... love. But I've only made things worse. I'm such a stupid, dumb and naive person. The worst person you could ever meet.

THE END

Milton Keynes UK
Ingram Content Group UK Ltd.
UKHW020006231024
449917UK00010B/547